The Book of
Little Folk

There are fairies at the bottom of our garden! (*from* Fairies *by Rose Fyleman*)

The Book of Little Folk

Faery Stories and Poems from Around the World

collected, retold, and illustrated by

Lauren Mills

Dial Books · *New York*

For Menkin Moler & Ninky Noodle

Published by Dial Books
A Division of Penguin Books USA Inc.
375 Hudson Street/New York, New York 10014
Copyright © 1997 by Lauren Mills Nolan
All rights reserved/Design by Amelia Lau Carling
Page 133 constitutes an extension of this copyright page.
Printed in the U.S.A. on acid-free paper
First Edition
1 3 5 7 9 10 8 6 4 2

Library of Congress Cataloging in Publication Data
Mills, Lauren A.
The book of little folk: faery stories and poems from around the world/
collected, retold, and illustrated by Lauren Mills.
—1st ed.   p.   cm.
Includes bibliographical references and index.
Summary: A collection of poems, short stories, folktales, and fairy
tales from a variety of cultures about these elusive and magical creatures.
ISBN 0-8037-1458-0 (trade)
1. Fairies—Literary collections.   [1. Fairies—Literary collections.]   I. Title
PZ5.M62Bo   1997   808.8′0375—dc20   96-22459   CIP   AC

The artwork was rendered in watercolors.

Note on the spelling of faery
In folklore the word *faery*, spelled with an *e*, usually encompasses all elves,
gnomes, and other enchanted little folk, whereas the word *fairy* specifically refers
to the diminutive winged faery, often female. I have used both spellings
in this book to preserve this distinction, though I have kept the traditional
spelling for *fairy tales*—whether or not they include fairies.

Contents

Foreword

Everyone has a passion, and as all my friends know, mine is the world of little folk. You can't step into my house without feeling that you've just crossed the border of Faeryland, for every corner is filled with some crafted fairy, gnome, or tomten. During the years I spent researching this book, my passion developed into a hopeless obsession, especially as I tried to determine the nature of these mysterious creatures.

Each time I thought I understood their place in folklore, I would be thrown off course by a report of an actual "sighting." A few friends confided to me that they had seen a gnome dart into a hole in a tree or garden. One woman swerved off the road in a snowstorm, and when she got out of her car she saw two little people laughing at her!

Do I believe in faeries? I would answer that question by saying that I believe in fairy tales. Folklorists and philosophers have long known that tales of little folk can be found in most, if not all, cultures of the world. These stories often carry similar themes, story lines, and characters. The universality of the tales and their enduring power to fascinate, satisfy, and comfort people everywhere have convinced me of their essential truths and importance. I am certainly not alone in my passion for this subject, as there exists an extensive body of popular and scholarly writing that classifies the little folk in a variety of ways and that offers a wide range of views on their nature, origin, and significance. To study the classifications and ancient folklore of little folk, readers may want to explore reference works by such authors as Briggs, Arrowsmith, and others listed in my bibliography.

As I gathered some of my favorite stories and poems of little folk from a variety of cultures for this book, I soon discovered the same basic stories cropping up in many different countries. The Irish story included in this collection, "Lusmore and the Fairies" (usually called "The Legend of Knockgrafton"), can also be found in Spain as "Toniño and the Fairies." The theme of a wee baby given as a gift to a barren woman wishing for a child is included in this collection as the English "Tom Thumb," the Japanese "Little One Inch," the Danish "Thumbelina," and the Mexican "Dwarf of Uxmal," but this theme can also be found in the Russian "Lipuniushka," the Jewish "K'ton ton," and the "Peach Boy" of Japan.

While some of these stories were surely carried across borders and over seas, how do we explain the similarity of tales that apparently evolved simultaneously in distant cultures? In 1880, folklorist Thomas Keightley wrote about this phenomenon: "We have seen that all these legendary beings and their characters and acts are remnants of ancient religious systems, the mental offspring of deep-thinking sages. . . . We find the same legends, modified also by circumstances, springing up in distant countries and amongst tribes and nations who could hardly have had any communication."

The twentieth-century philosopher Joseph Campbell attributed the similar themes and archetypes that occur in the myths of different cultures to the universal search for meaning in our lives. He believed that myths originate in our innermost needs and conflicts, acting as symbols and clues in our quest for spiritual truth. Calling a fairy tale a "child's myth," Campbell added, "There are proper myths for proper times of life. As you grow older, you need a sturdier mythology."

One might say then that a fairy tale serves as a stepping stone to later, more complicated beliefs about how to conduct our lives. The stories included in this collection of little but powerful hidden helpers such as the Swedish Tomten, the Russian Vasilisa's doll, the mischievous but helpful Hawaiian Menehunes, India's volatile Sir Buzz, and the naked elves in the Grimms' "Elves and the Shoemaker"—all might give to children the sense that there exists something outside of their day-to-day lives that can love and help them.

Stories like these are quite different from religious lessons, or even classical myths of superheroes, in that they are more accessible to a child. The little folk themselves take on the characteristics of children with all their imperfections, their tempers and naughtiness, their endearing proportions, and especially their love of play. Their magical attributes give them their otherworldly qualities, but their charming diminutive size brings them down to earth—closer to the toads and mice that so often populate their stories. Thus, tales of little folk who aid the "good" child may serve as the first symbols of an unseen higher power. Instilled early enough, this belief can last a lifetime. As psychologist Bruno Bettelheim said in his book *The Uses of Enchantment*, "Far from making demands (as myths do), the fairy tale reassures, gives hope for the future, and holds out the promise of a happy ending. That is why Lewis Carroll called it a love-gift."

Bettelheim felt that fairy tales deal with important conflicts and fears already within a child, but offer satisfying solutions in simple symbolic language that can be interpreted according to the needs of the listener. A child knows that there are no evil giants but that there *are* evil grown-ups. It is actually less scary to hear a story about an evil giant than to hear or see in the news a true story about an evil grown-up.

I would go farther and say that if a giant is an exaggerated symbol of a grown-up, then many of the stories of little folk, especially those about tiny children such as "Thumbelina" and "Little One Inch," are exaggerated symbols of childhood. The message instilled by such tales is that even a fellow no more than an inch high can succeed against all odds in a huge and terrifying world if he perseveres, is good, and has faith. These are empowering tales for those who feel powerless.

Stories of little folk have been passed down orally from generation to generation for centuries, as if they were old, treasured remedies for the mind and soul. Research has shown they are just that, for they spark the imagination—an important tool for creativity and problem-solving. According to Dr. Karen N. Olness of the Minneapolis Children's Medical Center, when young children listen to fairy tales, they develop the image-making skills that are the foundation of learning. Writing of the importance of spontaneous imagery and playfulness in children's development, Olness has described the body of the folklore of little people as "a history of imagery handed down through generations." Sadly, higher-level thinking and comprehension are stunted when the imagination is not developed in the early years. Books by educators Jane M. Healy and Joseph Chilton Pearce relay the heartbreaking discovery of the damage to the mind that occurs among students in our technological society, where push-button entertainment has largely replaced traditional storytelling and playtime.

While of more ancient origin, tales of little folk gained an enduring place in Western European literature during the Industrial Revolution, beginning with the publication of the Grimms' first volume of folktales in 1812. Fantasy and fairy tales later became the subject matter for prominent Victorian artists and authors such as illustrator Arthur Rackham and poet William Butler Yeats. Though the belief in faeries has certainly begun to weaken in our technological age, interest in their tales is still evident in the abundance of volumes of fairy tales published for children in recent years. It seems that when society veers from what is innately human and close to the earth, we seek the faeries again. Or could it be that the faeries—those offspring of the human imagination— seek *us*? Perhaps in exploring the world of faery we are validating our imagination, the most magical and mysterious part of our being.

Joseph Campbell believed that fairy tales are often about children being "stuck," afraid of making that heroic and miraculous transformation from childhood to adulthood. Children, knowing that fairy tales are for *them*, often ask me why I am "stuck" on writing about and painting fairies, elves, and other little folk. I tell them that I clearly remember making a wish when I was very young: to grow up to the age of eight and no older. I have heard that it is after this age that the belief in magic disappears. So I believe that there must have been some playful faery, a muse perhaps, who granted my wish by hiding herself in the part of me that forever lives in that enchanted land of little folk.

That was my wish as a child. And now my wish as a grown-up is to give children images of little folk, through words and pictures, that will ignite their imaginations, fill their souls, comfort their hearts, and enrich their inheritance with the ancient wisdom of this world's many fascinating cultures. It is my "love-gift."

Fairy Bread

Come up here, O dusty feet!
  Here is fairy bread to eat.
Here in my retiring room,
  Children, you may dine
On the golden smell of broom
  And the shade of pine;
And when you have eaten well,
Fairy stories hear and tell.

—Robert Louis Stevenson
Scottish, 1850–1894

The Little Elf

I met a little Elf Man, once,
Down where the lilies blow.
I asked him why he was so small,
And why he didn't grow.

He slightly frowned, and with his eye
He looked me through and through.
"I'm quite as big for me," said he,
"As you are big for you."

—John Kendrick Bangs
American, 1862–1922

Leelinau
Native North American/Ojibwa

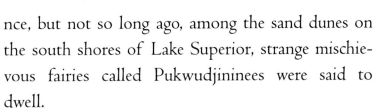

nce, but not so long ago, among the sand dunes on the south shores of Lake Superior, strange mischievous fairies called Pukwudjininees were said to dwell.

The Ojibwa people knew of them because there is a certain little lake not far back from the Great Lake, on the shores of which the fairies' tracks could be plainly seen. These tracks were no bigger than children's footprints. Not only that, but in the manito wac, or Spirit Wood, their gleeful voices could be heard.

Oh, some attributed the sound to the buzzing of bees; for certainly, if you were to drowse at the wood's edge, you might indeed hear lilting sounds high in the pines like the gentle, musical drone of insects telling secrets you may never learn. But it was not the bees the people heard; it was the Pukwudjininees. And it was the playful Pukwudjininees who sometimes stole a fisherman's paddle just for sheer merriment, or plucked a feather from the hair of a sleeping hunter, or pilfered a piece of skin from his coat. And when the hunter awoke, he would hear snickering in the leaves.

Leelinau was the young daughter of a chief in the dune country, and she was fond of lonely walks. She did not heed the warnings of her parents, who told her that there was no telling what else the Pukwudjininees

3

might steal—perhaps they might take a human child, just for fun. The dreamy-eyed Leelinau would venture into places where even brave warriors dared not go.

One day she happened upon some little tracks in the sand. Placing her own foot inside one, she found it fit perfectly. Delighting in this, she followed the tracks into the Spirit Wood.

Leelinau was missing from the village the whole day, and upon her return in the evening she told her people of the enchanting time she had spent with some strange little folk; and how they led her into the heart of the forest, where they sang and danced with her and fed her on new and delicate food.

Her mother and father were alarmed to hear this and forbade her ever to go to that wood again. As time went on, they had more reason to be anxious. Since her visit to the Spirit Wood, Leelinau grew no taller, and her behavior was odd as well. Often she could be found sitting in the dirt talking to squirrels or woodchucks, braiding tiny strands of her hair for birds' nests, feeding honey to the butterflies, and even whispering to the flowers! Leelinau knew things about the trees, insects, and stars that even the medicine man did not know; and she never seemed content to be with the other girls, but rather pined away for a place she called the "happy land," where she said there was no fighting or crying, and no hunting or death.

The others laughed at her for acting so foolishly toward the animals; for only eating maize, roots, and fruit, and refusing to feast on the deer the hunters brought back. With anger flashing in her eyes Leelinau declared that the animals had just as much right to live as they, or the Creator would not have made them; and furthermore, that the shedding of one another's blood by men was foolish, so long as they had room in which to live apart in peace. She said that the happy land was filled only with love and kindness, and that those little people she had seen in the

They led her into the heart of the forest, where they sang and danced with her.

wood might be messengers from that land.

As time passed, it was plain to all that the fairies had cast their spell on Leelinau. For by now she was a young lady, yet she still remained as small and slender as a little child. The people could not help but admire her, though. She had the most pleasing sylphlike features, with very bright black eyes and tiny feet, and she walked and leapt with the grace of a young doe. One young hunter was so taken by her beauty that he asked to marry her.

Leelinau's father agreed at once, for who else would have her? She was beautiful, no doubt, but so small and so strange. Leelinau's mother said, "Perhaps a marriage bond will break this hold the little people have over her and bring her back to her senses. It is our only hope."

So Leelinau was told to marry the hunter, and the marriage arrangements were made. She was arrayed in the finest of clothes, with shells and quills embroidered in her dress and wildflowers adorning her hair. All declared that never was there a prettier bride in the dune country, and her parents smiled at her proudly.

"This one last wish I ask," said Leelinau, looking up at her father with round, pleading eyes.

"Anything for you," he said.

"Grant that I may walk alone one last time by the Spirit Wood," she said.

Perhaps it was her eyes that cast a spell over her father. For whatever reason, he gave her his permission, adding, "But you must come back soon. The moment you do, the ceremony will start. Hurry now, we shall all be waiting, dear one."

Leelinau embraced her parents more tenderly than ever before. Then she ran off. They all waited eagerly for her, but they waited in vain. Leelinau never returned.

A fisherman said he had seen one of the Pukwudjininees step out of the wood to meet her in the twilight, and that he recognized the being as the Fairy Prince of the Green Pines, the tallest of his tribe. He wore pine plumes on his head and placed a spray of pine in Leelinau's hair. He took his bride's hand and led the maiden away, away to the happy land, the people say; for never again was Leelinau seen on the south shores of Lake Superior.

The Fairy Dance

The soft stars are shining,
The moon is alight;
The folk of the forest
Are dancing tonight:
O swift and gay
Is the song that they sing;
They float and sway
As they dance in a ring.

O seek not to find them,
The wee folk so fair;
They're shy as the swallow
And swift as the air:
If you come, they are gone
Like a snowflake in May;
Like a breath, like a sigh,
They vanish away.

—Katherine Davis
American, 1892–1980

Lusmore and the Fairies

Irish

t the foot of the gloomy Galtee Mountains there once lived a poor little man with a gigantic hump on his back that weighed so heavily upon him, he looked like a gnarled tree limb bent over with some odd burden. He was a gentle soul, though, and always wore a sprig of lusmore, or foxglove, in his cap. On account of this, some called him "Lusmore." Others, repelled by his grotesque shape, called him cruel names unbefitting his sweet nature. In truth, they were jealous of him because he could plait straw rushes into fine hats and baskets that fetched higher prices than their own. They liked to make up stories about him, saying that he knew the magic powers of herbs and used them in witchcraft.

Be that as it may, it happened that Lusmore was returning one evening from the pretty town of Cahir. Due to the weight of his great hump, he found walking difficult, so it was not until dark that he reached the old prehistoric mound of Knockgrafton. Weary as he was, and discouraged by the distance he still had to travel, he sat down by the mound to rest and gazed mournfully at the moon.

Presently he heard a beautiful but unearthly song rising from the mound. The voices pleased him, and he might have been content to listen to them forever if it were not for the fact that they repeated themselves over and over. Lusmore soon tired of hearing the same verse sung again and again:

9

"Mondays, Tuesdays, oh, such pretty days!
Mondays, Tuesdays, oh, such pretty days!"

Over and over they sang this verse with not a change, and so when at last there came a pause, Lusmore, who had listened carefully to the tune and could sing quite well himself, added in perfect pitch and rhythm:

"And I also love Wednesdays!"

Then he continued singing along with the voices in the mound, again adding his part at the pause.

Well, the fairies, for it was they whom he had heard, were delighted with Lusmore's addition to their song. His skill at singing was not over-looked either. They decided to bring the mortal among them and did so with the speed of a whirlwind.

Lusmore had never seen such a glorious sight as he twirled down into the fairies' mound and landed as softly as a piece of straw on the floor of their great hall. The fairies paid him the greatest honor, placing him above all the musicians and waiting upon him as if he were king of the land.

Before long, Lusmore saw a great discussion among the fairies, and he became quite frightened; for one can never be certain what tricks the fairies may play. Then one fairy stepped forward and said to him:

"Lusmore! Lusmore!
Doubt not, nor deplore,
For that hump which you bore
On your back is no more;
Look down on the floor,
And view it, Lusmore!"

He became quite frightened; for one can never be certain what tricks the fairies may play.

As soon as these words were spoken, Lusmore's hump tumbled to the floor of the mound and he stood up tall with a strange feeling of lightness he had never known before. Cautiously he lifted his head, half expecting he would topple backward as before, but instead he could finally see up above and all around him. He was so thrilled to be rid of his hump that he could have jumped over the moon like the old cow in the riddle. Everything seemed so beautiful that he grew dizzy with delight. At last he sat, his eyelids shut, and Lusmore fell into a deep sleep.

When he awoke, he was sitting in the same spot he had been in the night before, but now the cows and sheep were grazing about him and the sun was up. Lusmore said his prayers before carefully feeling his back, testing to see if he had just been dreaming. But no, the hump was truly gone, and more than that, the fairies had clad him in a full new suit of clothes, so that Lusmore was now a well-shaped dapper fellow!

As you might guess, he skipped and danced all the way home. Not a soul he met knew him without his hump, and he had the most difficult time persuading them that he was, indeed, the same man, at least on the inside.

The story of Lusmore's hump began to spread, of course, from town to town, until one day a woman and her son visited Lusmore. The son was a humpback just as Lusmore had been, but he did not have Lusmore's sweet and gentle nature. No, he was spiteful and mean; nevertheless, when he asked how, exactly, Lusmore got the fairies to remove his hump, Lusmore told him what he wanted to know.

Jack Madden, for that was the humpback's name, went to the mound at Knockgrafton at nightfall and waited there. Soon enough he heard the fairies sing their verse, along with Lusmore's addition:

"Mondays, Tuesdays, oh, such pretty days!
And I also love Wednesdays!"

Now, Jack Madden did not listen carefully to the tune as Lusmore had, nor did he wait for the fairies to pause. He was in such a hurry to be rid of his hump that he rudely interrupted the song with not an ounce of grace or rhythm. He sang, if it could be called singing:

"And then come Thursday and Friday too!"

He added an extra day to the song, reasoning that if one worked, two would be even better; and if Lusmore were given one new suit of clothes, he should be given two. Well, no sooner were Jack's words out than he was whisked into the mound with the force of a tornado. A host of angry fairies whirled around him screeching, "Who ruined our song? Who ruined our song?" One fairy stepped out of the crowd and said:

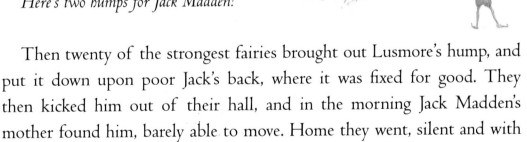

"Jack Madden! Jack Madden!
Your words came so bad in
The tune we felt glad in;
This castle you're had in,
That your life we may sadden;
Here's two humps for Jack Madden!"

Then twenty of the strongest fairies brought out Lusmore's hump, and put it down upon poor Jack's back, where it was fixed for good. They then kicked him out of their hall, and in the morning Jack Madden's mother found him, barely able to move. Home they went, silent and with downcast hearts.

Jack died soon after, leaving a heavy curse to anyone who would dare to go singing with the fairies! As for Lusmore, he married and had many children who loved to listen to his songs—especially the tune he helped the fairies sing.

The Lepracaun

I caught him at work one day, myself,
   In the castle-ditch, where foxglove grows,—
A wrinkled, wizen'd and bearded Elf,
   Spectacles stuck on his pointed nose,
   Silver buckles to his hose,
   Leather apron—shoe in his lap—
     "Rip-rap, tip-tap,
     Tick-tack-too!
(A grasshopper on my cap!
   Away the moth flew!)
Buskins for a fairy prince,
   Brogues for his son,—
Pay me well, pay me well,
   When the job is done!"

The rogue was mine, beyond a doubt.
I stared at him; he stared at me;
"Servant, Sir!" "Humph!" says he,
        And pull'd a snuff-box out.
He took a long pinch, look'd better pleased,
        The queer little Lepracaun;
Offer'd the box with a whimsical grace,—
Pouf! he flung the dust in my face,
        And, while I sneezed,
                Was gone!

—William Allingham
Irish, 1824–1889
Excerpt from The Lepracaun

Thumbelina

Danish

by Hans Christian Andersen, 1805–1875

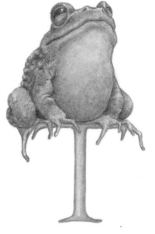

here was once a woman who dearly wanted a wee child of her own, but she had no idea where to find one. So she went to an old witch and said to her: "I would so much like to have a tiny child; do please tell me where I can find one."

"A tiny child? Pff! Nothing is easier. Take this barleycorn. Now mind you, it's not the kind the farmer sows in his field or feeds to his chickens. No, this is a special seed. Plant it in a flowerpot, and then see what happens!"

"Oh, thank you!" said the woman, and gave the witch a coin. Then she went straight home and planted the barleycorn. In no time there grew a lovely flower quite like a tulip, only its petals were shut tight, as if it were just a bud.

"Well, it is pretty anyway," said the woman, and kissed the red and yellow petals; but the moment she kissed them, the flower burst open with a pop. Indeed, it was plainly a tulip; but that was not all. There in the center of the blossom sat a tiny girl! She was as delicate and pretty as could be; and as she was not half as big as the woman's thumb, she was named Thumbelina.

An elegantly polished walnut shell served as Thumbelina's bed, blue violet petals were her mattress, and a rose leaf was her blanket. There she slept at night, but during the day she played about on the tabletop, where the woman had set a bowl ringed by a garland of flowers. Their stems dipped down into the water, and in the middle a large tulip petal floated. Here Thumbelina liked to sit and row herself from one side of the bowl to the other, using two white horse hairs as oars. It was the most charming sight! And then, how she sang—Oh! with the sweetest voice that has ever been heard!

One night while Thumbelina lay sleeping in her pretty bed, a hideous toad came hopping in through a broken windowpane and landed right next to Thumbelina!

She would make such a nice wife for my son, thought the toad. And so she snatched up the walnut shell in which Thumbelina lay sleeping and hopped off with it, through the window and down into the garden.

There flowed a wide brook, and its banks were marshy and muddy: Here the toad lived with her son. Ugh! He was warty and clumsy, just like his mother. "Koax, koax, brekke-ke-kex!" was all he could say when he saw the pretty little girl in the walnut shell.

"Ssh! Not so loud or you'll wake her," said the old toad. "She could escape from us yet, for she's as light as swan's down. Let's put her out on one of the lily pads. It will be an island to her since she's so small; she cannot escape there, and in the meantime we'll fix up the best room under the mud for you two to live in."

There grew a great many water lilies in the brook, with their broad green leaves floating on the surface. It happened that the largest of these was the farthest away, but still the old toad swam out and placed the walnut shell on it with Thumbelina sleeping inside.

Poor little Thumbelina woke up very early the next morning, and when she saw where she was, she began to cry bitterly; for on all sides of the great green leaf there was water, and no way for her to reach land.

The old toad was down in the mud decorating the room with rushes

"Allow me to introduce my son to you."

and water lilies to make it cozy for her new daughter-in-law. Then she and her ugly son swam out to the water lily where Thumbelina was, for they meant to fetch her pretty bed and place it in the bridal chamber before bringing Thumbelina there.

The old mother toad curtsied to her and said, "Allow me to introduce my son to you. He is to be your husband, and we shall all live together in a lovely home in the mud."

"Koax, koax, brekke-ke-kex!" was all the son could say. Then they took her cradle and swam away with it, while Thumbelina sat all alone on the green leaf and cried, for she did not want to live with the horrible toad or marry her ugly son.

The little fish that swam down in the water had seen the old toad and heard what she said. They were curious to have a look at the girl, so they poked their heads out of the water. The moment they saw Thumbelina, they thought her so pretty; and they couldn't bear to think that she must live under the mud with the toads. No, that must never be! So they swarmed together in the water around the green stalk of the lily pad, and gnawed on it with their teeth until they freed the leaf. It floated quietly away, carrying Thumbelina far down the stream where the old mother toad and her son could not reach her.

Thumbelina sailed past many places, and the little birds perched in the bushes saw her and sang out, "What a pretty little maiden." The leaf carried her farther and farther on, until at last she was in a foreign land.

A dainty little white butterfly fluttered 'round and 'round Thumbelina, for it had taken a great liking to her; and she too was pleased. By now the toad could not come near her, and the countryside to which she had come was so lovely. The sun shone on the water and gleamed like the finest gold. Presently she took off her sash and tied one end around the butterfly. The other end she bound to the lily pad, and standing on the leaf she glided across the water more swiftly than ever.

Just then a big June bug came flying near, and catching sight of Thumbelina, clasped its claws around her slender waist and flew up with her into a tree. But the green lily pad floated down the river and the white butterfly with it, for it was tied to the leaf and could not get loose.

Poor Thumbelina was terrified, but she was even more miserable at the thought of the pretty white butterfly. Unless it could manage to free itself, it would surely starve to death. But this did not worry the June bug in the least. It settled itself next to Thumbelina, fed her some nectar from the blossoms of the tree, and said that she was very pretty, although she did not look at all like a June bug.

Before long, all the other June bugs that lived in the tree came to pay a visit; they looked at Thumbelina, and the lady June bugs examined her with their antennae and said, "Why, she has only two legs, what a pitiable sight!" "She has no antennae!" said the others. "She has such a thin body. Ugh, she looks almost human! Oh, how ugly!" cried all the lady June bugs.

The one who had carried her off still thought she was pretty, but since the others all were agreeing that she was the ugliest thing they'd ever seen, at length he began to think so too and would have nothing to do with her; she could go where she liked. They flew with her down from the tree and sat her on a daisy. There she wept, because she was so ugly that the

June bugs couldn't stand to look at her; and all the time she was really as beautiful as one might ever imagine, as exquisite as the finest rose petal!

All summer long poor Thumbelina lived alone in that enormous wood. She wove herself a bed of grass and hung it under a large dock leaf to protect it from the rain. She ate from the nectar of the flowers and drank from the morning dew on the leaves; and so passed the summer and the fall. Then along came winter—the long, cold winter.

All the birds who had sung so sweetly for her had now flown away; the trees dropped their leaves, the flowers died; the great dock leaf under which she had lived shriveled up, and nothing remained of it but the withered stalk. She felt bitterly cold, for by this time her clothes were in tatters, and poor Thumbelina herself was so delicate and tiny that she almost froze to death. It began to snow, and every snowflake that fell upon her was just like a huge shovelful would be to us, for we are quite big and she was smaller than a thumb. So she wrapped herself up in a dead leaf, but there was no warmth in that, and she trembled with cold.

On the edge of the wood lay a large cornfield; but the corn had long been harvested, and only the bare stubble still stood above the frozen ground. This made an entire forest for her to walk through, and how she shivered with the cold!

At length she came to the door of the field mouse who had a little hole down below the stubble. There the field mouse lived warm and snug, with a storeroom full of grain, a cozy kitchen and parlor. Poor Thumbelina stood outside the door as wretched as any beggar-child and asked for a piece of barleycorn, for she had not a bite to eat for two whole days.

"You poor little thing!" said the field mouse, for she was at heart a kindly old soul. "Come inside my warm home and share my dinner."

As she was at once pleased with Thumbelina, she made a suggestion. "You're quite welcome to stay with me for the winter, as far as I'm concerned, just as long as you keep my rooms nice and tidy and tell me stories, for I'm so fond of them." And Thumbelina did as the good old field mouse asked and felt quite comfortable there.

"I daresay we shall have a visitor before long," said the field mouse. "My neighbor generally pays me a visit once a week. He is even better off than I am. He has a much finer house, with a great many large rooms, and goes about in a splendid black velvet coat. If only you could get him for a husband, you would be well taken care of. But his sight is very bad. You must tell him all the prettiest stories you know." Thumbelina took no notice of this talk of marriage, for the neighbor was a mole. He came and paid them a visit in his black velvet coat.

He was rich and well-educated too, according to the field mouse. "His house is twenty times larger than mine," she said. He was very learned, but he couldn't stand sunshine or flowers; he poked all sorts of fun at them, never having seen them.

Thumbelina had to sing to him, so she sang both, "Ladybug, Ladybug, fly away home" and "Ring around the roses," so prettily that the mole fell in love with her; but he did not say anything, as he was much too cautious a mole for that.

He had lately dug a long underground passage from his house to theirs. Here the field mouse and Thumbelina were invited to stroll as they pleased. He told them, however, not to be afraid of the dead bird that lay in the passage; it was a whole bird with beak and feathers and must have just died as winter began, and was now buried in the very spot where he had built his tunnel.

The mole took a bit of touchwood in his mouth, for it shines in the dark just like fire, and went ahead to give them light in the long, dark tunnel. When they came to where the dead bird lay, the mole tilted his long nose up and thrust it through the roof, making a hole so that the daylight could shine down. In the middle of the passage lay a dead swallow with its pretty wings folded close to its sides, and head and legs tucked in beneath its feathers; the poor bird must have died of the cold. Thumbelina felt sorry for it, for she dearly loved the birds who had sung and twittered for her so sweetly all summer long. But the mole kicked at it with his bandy legs, saying, "Now it will twitter no more! How wretched it must be to be born a bird. Thank goodness no child of mine will ever be one. A bird like that has nothing but its twittering, and then he's sure to starve to death when winter comes."

"Just what I'd expect to hear from a sensible man like you," said the field mouse. "What does a bird have with all its singing when it's only bound to starve and freeze?"

Thumbelina didn't say a word, but when the other two had turned their backs to the swallow, she bent down and brushed aside the feathers from his head and kissed his closed eyes gently. Perhaps it was he who sang so sweetly in the summer, she thought. How much joy he gave me.

The mole now closed up the hole he had made in the roof and saw the two ladies home. But that night Thumbelina could not sleep; so she got out of bed and wove a nice big blanket of hay, which she carried down and spread over the dead swallow, and she took some soft thistledown that she had found in the field mouse's storeroom and tucked this in at his sides so that the bird might lie warm in the cold earth.

"Good-bye, dear bird," she said. "Good-bye, and thank you for your beautiful singing last summer when all the trees were green and the sun shone so warmly on us." Then she laid her head against the bird's breast. But at that moment she had quite a fright, for she heard a thumping inside! It was the swallow's heart. The bird was not dead, only numb and unconscious; and now that she had warmed him, he was coming to life again.

In autumn the swallows all fly away to the warm countries, but if one is late in starting and lags behind, it gets so stiff from the cold that it falls down as if dead. There it lies where it fell, and the cold snow covers it over.

Thumbelina trembled from her fright, for the bird was so large in comparison to herself who was only an inch high. She took courage, however, and tucked the thistledown still more closely around the poor swallow and fetched her own bedcover and spread this over the bird.

The next night she crept out again to the bird, and found him alive, but very weak; he could only open his eyes for a moment to look at Thumbelina, who was standing there with a bit of touchwood in her hand, for she had no other lantern.

"Thank you, dear little child," the sick swallow said to her. "I am so beautifully warm now. I shall soon get my strength back and will be able to fly again, out into the warm sunshine!"

"Oh!" she said, "it is very cold outside, snowing and freezing. Stay in your warm bed and I will take care of you."

Then she brought him water in a flower petal, which he drank. Afterward he told her how he had torn his wing on a bramble, so that he could not keep up with the other swallows when they flew far away to the warm countries. At last he had fallen to the ground, but he could remember no more.

The whole winter long the swallow stayed there, and Thumbelina took tender care of him. Neither the mole nor the field mouse were told anything about it, for they had nothing but dislike for the poor swallow.

As soon as the spring arrived, and the sun began to warm the earth, the swallow said good-bye to Thumbelina, who opened the hole in the roof for him. The sun shone in delightfully, and the swallow asked Thumbelina if she would come with him; she could sit on his back. Thumbelina wanted very much to fly far out into the green woods, but she knew it would grieve the old field mouse to be left like that.

"No, I cannot," said Thumbelina.

"Good-bye then, good-bye, you dear, sweet girl," said the swallow, as it flew toward the open sunshine. Thumbelina gazed after him with tears filling her eyes, for she was so fond of the swallow.

"Tweet, tweet!" sang the bird, and flew off into the woods.

Thumbelina was terribly sad. She was not allowed to go out into the warm sunshine. The corn that had been sown in the earth above the field mouse's burrow had now grown high in the air, making a thick forest for the tiny girl.

"During the summer you must prepare for your wedding," the field mouse said to her, "for our neighbor, the mole, has made his marriage proposal. How lucky for a poor girl like you! Now, you will need both woolens and linens if you are to be the mole's wife."

Thumbelina had to spend all her days spinning, and the field mouse also hired four spiders to spin and weave for her day and night. Every evening the mole would visit, and go on and on about how when the summer was over, the sun would not be nearly as warm, whereas now it scorched the earth till it was as hard as stone. Yes, and when the summer had ended, then he would have his wedding with Thumbelina. But she was not at all pleased, for she found the mole to be a terrible bore.

Every morning as the sun rose, and every evening as it set, she slipped out the door, and when the wind parted the ears of corn so that she could glimpse the blue sky, she thought of how beautiful and bright it was out there, and wished to see her dear swallow just once more. But the swallow never came; certainly he had flown far away, far into the beautiful green forest.

Autumn arrived, and Thumbelina's wedding things were ready. "In four weeks you will be married!" the field mouse said to her. But Thumbelina wept and said she would not marry the boring mole.

"Piff, sniff!" said the field mouse. "Don't be so stubborn, or I'll bite you with my white teeth. He's a fine husband, he is. The Queen herself hasn't anything to compare with that black velvet coat. His kitchen and cellar are full, and you should be thankful for that."

Well, the wedding day arrived, and the mole came to fetch Thumbelina. She would have to live with him down under the earth and never come into the warm sunshine, for that he could not stand. The poor girl was full of sorrow, for she now had to say farewell to the beautiful sun. And as she begged so hard, the field mouse gave her leave to go to the door to do so.

"Good-bye, bright sun," she said sadly, and stretching out her arms to it, she took a few steps outside the field mouse's doorway; for the corn had once again been cut and only the short, dry stubble remained. "Good-bye, good-bye," she said, throwing her tiny arms 'round a little red flower that stood near. "Remember me to the dear swallow, if you chance to see him."

"Tweet, tweet!" she suddenly heard above her. She looked up and there was the swallow, just overhead. As soon as he saw Thumbelina, he was delighted. She told her old friend how unwilling she was to marry the dreadful mole and to live deep underground, where the sun never shone. As she spoke, she could not stop from crying.

"The cold winter is coming," said the swallow. "I am flying far away to warmer lands. Won't you come with me now? You can sit on my back, and we will fly far away from the ugly mole and his dark house, over the mountains to the warm countries where the sun shines more brightly than it does here, where it is always summer, and there are beautiful flowers. Do come with me, dear little Thumbelina, who saved my life when I lay frozen in the dark tunnel."

"Yes, I will go with you!" Thumbelina said, and climbed on the swallow's back, her feet resting on his outstretched wings. She tied her sash to one of his strongest feathers, and up the swallow flew, high into the air, over the woods and over the sea, high up above the tall mountains where the snow forever lies. And if she was cold, she snuggled down under his warm feathers, only putting her head out to see all the beauty of the world beneath her.

At last they reached the warm land, where the sun shone more brightly than Thumbelina had ever seen it. The sky seemed twice as high, and in the hedges grew the finest green and purple grapes; in the groves hung oranges and lemons; the air smelled sweetly of myrtle and curled mint; and the most delightful children darted about on the paths, playing with gayly colored butterflies. But the swallow kept flying on and on, and the country became more and more beautiful. Then under leafy green trees and beside a blue lake stood an ancient castle built of gleaming white marble. Vines twisted around the high pillars: On the topmost of these were many swallows' nests, and in one of them dwelt the swallow who was carrying Thumbelina.

"Here is my house!" said the swallow. "But if you would rather have a

home of your own, all you need do is choose one of the fine flowers that grows below, and I will set you upon it. There you shall have a cozy place to live."

"That would be wonderful!" said Thumbelina, and clapped her hands.

There lay a great white pillar which had fallen to the ground and broken into three pieces; among these grew the most exquisite large white flowers.

The swallow flew down with Thumbelina and set her upon one of the broad petals—but how astonished she was! There in the middle of the flower sat a little man. He wore a lovely crown on his head and bright wings on his shoulders, and he was no bigger than Thumbelina. He was the fairy of the flower. In every flower lived such a man or woman, but this was the king of them all.

"Goodness, how very handsome he is," whispered Thumbelina to the swallow.

The little king was terribly frightened by the swallow, for in comparison to him, who was so very small, the bird seemed gigantic. But when he caught sight of Thumbelina, he was delighted; for she was the most beautiful girl he had ever seen. And so he took his crown from his head and placed it on hers, asking to know her name and whether she would be his wife. If so, she would be queen of all the flowers.

Yes, he would make a proper sort of husband for her, different from a toad's son, or a mole with a black velvet coat. So she said yes to the handsome king, and out from every flower stepped a lady or gentleman so charming that it was a pleasure to see them. Each brought Thumbelina a present, but the best of all was a beautiful pair of wings which were fastened to her back, so now she too could fly from flower to flower. How delightful! The swallow sat above in his nest and sang to them as well as he could, but his heart was full of sorrow, for he was fond of Thumbelina and did not want to be parted from her.

"You should not be called Thumbelina," said the fairy of the flower to her. "It is an ugly name, and you are so beautiful. We shall call you Maia."

In time the swallow called to her, "Good-bye, good-bye," and flew away again from the warm lands, far, far away to Denmark. Here he had a little nest above the window of a room where there lived a man who could tell fairy tales. The swallow sang to him—"Tweet, tweet!" And that is where this whole story comes from.

Fairies

There are fairies at the bottom of our garden!
    It's not so very, very far away;
You pass the gardener's shed and you just keep straight
       ahead—
    I do so hope they've really come to stay.
There's a little wood, with moss in it and beetles,
    And a little stream that quietly runs through;
You wouldn't think they'd dare to come merrymaking
       there—
          Well, they do.

There are fairies at the bottom of our garden!
    They often have a dance on summer nights;
The butterflies and bees make a lovely little breeze,
    And the rabbits stand about and hold the lights.
Did you know that they could sit upon the moonbeams
    And pick a little star to make a fan,
And dance away up there in the middle of the air?
          Well, they can.

There are fairies at the bottom of our garden!
    You cannot think how beautiful they are;
They all stand up and sing when the Fairy Queen
       and King
    Come gently floating down upon their car.
The King is very proud and *very* handsome;
    The Queen—now can you guess who that could be
(She's a little girl all day, but at night she steals away)?
          Well—it's ME!

—Rose Fyleman
English, 1877–1957

The Dwarf of Uxmal

Mexican / Mayan

here once was an old woman who lived deep in the jungle of the Yucatán in Mexico. The Yucatán is a very hot place where birds with large hooked beaks the colors of rainbows fly about freely. Vines twist up the trees and gigantic snakes with scales that glitter like jewels hang from the drooping branches. On the outskirts of the jungle was the city of Uxmal (pronounced *oosh-mal*), where the trees were chopped down and the people lived in homes of stone and mud, safe from the thick jungle where the jaguar and iguana would prowl amongst the twisted trees and the colorful birds and the hanging snakes. But the old woman who lived in the jungle knew its ways, and was not afraid.

The old woman was said to have magical powers, and because she was withered and strange-looking, the people called her "witch," and did not dare speak to her. And so the animals were her friends, yet she still longed for something more, a child, someone of her own kind.

Now, one day a snake brought her an oddly spotted egg. It was rather large, even larger than the eggs the tortoise lays. So the old woman did not eat it. No, she put it in her gourd pot and prayed. And then three weeks later she heard the egg crack and a little cry come from the pot. She looked in and there sat a tiny baby boy! Well, the old woman was more than delighted and knew just what to do. She rocked him, and sang to him, and fed him, and bathed him. All the things a good mother would do she did for him.

When he grew a bit older, she taught him the wisdom of the animals and trees. She showed him how the animals do not take more than they need, for if they did there would not be enough for them in the end. "The jaguar makes his meal from the slowest and weakest of deer," she said, "so that only the strongest deer live to make strong babies. And so the jaguar helps the deer."

The little boy grew wiser as he grew older, but at his full height he was still only the size of a three-year-old child! He was strong and brave though, and rode on the back of the jaguar and tumbled with the snake.

The village children befriended the boy dwarf, for he was quite kind and gentle and knew how to keep them from quarreling. Then it was not long before the rest of the villagers came to the little dwarf with questions or troubles. The "dwarf wizard," as they called him, was more wise and fair than their king, who sat lazily in the temple all day, caring little for his people. When there was an argument between two villagers and it was brought before the king to judge who was right and who was wrong, the king favored the one who had given him the better gift, even if that one was in the wrong. And this is why the villagers hated the king and would go to the dwarf wizard instead.

When the king heard about the dwarf wizard, he was filled with jealousy and devised a plan to ruin him. He summoned the dwarf to him and said, "If you are truly a wizard, then build a temple next to mine in one night. If it is here when I wake up, you shall take my place as king. If you cannot do it, then you shall die."

The poor dwarf went home to his mother and said sadly, "Mother, I shall die, for this task is impossible."

But his wise mother said, "It is surely impossible if you do not try. Here, form this cornmeal into tiny bricks and build a small model of a temple. Make it fit for a king, then bring it quickly to the place where the temple is to be built."

Then the dwarf's mother summoned all the animals of the jungle, the colorful birds, the gigantic snakes, the jaguars and tortoises, the lizards, deer, and even the bees and ants. She summoned the people of Uxmal too, the young and the old. They each carried stone and mud, as much as their backs could hold, to where the dwarf had set the model of the temple. And then they all began to build a huge temple according to the model the dwarf had built.

Now, perhaps the dwarf's mother *was* a witch or sorceress of sorts, for the king did not wake the next day nor the next, and neither the people nor the animals tired of working. Day after day, the king slept as the people and the animals worked together building the temple, and to all of them it seemed as if only one night had passed when they were finished.

The king woke as if it were the next morning and was amazed to find the beautiful temple there. It was a steep pyramid, and on top was a house with richly decorated rooms and an elephant's head carved over the entrance. He pretended to be pleased, but he was secretly enraged and devised another plan to kill the dwarf.

Then the dwarf's mother summoned all the animals of the jungle.

"Congratulations, little dwarf, now you shall take my throne and rule Uxmal and all of the Yucatán, for you are truly a wizard and fit for my post. But first there shall be a ceremony before you can be king. I shall crack six cocoyole nuts on your head."

The dwarf paled and said, "My skull may be hard, but I doubt that it will stand the thumping."

"Pah! What is a mere ceremony? Surely the throne is worth a twinge," said the king. "We shall hold the ceremony tomorrow morning or you shall not take my place."

So once more the dwarf went home to his mother and said sadly, "Mother, I shall surely die with the first blow of the cocoyole nut, for my skull is not hard enough for that."

But his wise mother said, "You shall surely die unless we make your skull hard enough." And so she cut off her son's hair and saved it. She took downy feathers from the birds and wax from the bees and put that on the dwarf's head as a soft cushion. And then, with more wax from the bees, she glued the old shell of a small tortoise on top of the feathers. Then she glued his hair on top of the tortoiseshell in such a clever way that no one could tell what she had done.

In the morning the old woman said to her son, "Go now to the king and tell him in front of all his people that you will be glad to go through his nut-cracking ceremony if he, in turn, will allow you to crack six cocoyole nuts over his head afterward."

So the dwarf did just what his mother told him to do, and the king laughed but agreed; for he planned on killing the dwarf with the first blow. The first nut cracked, and then the second and the third . . . all six cocoyole nuts cracked without the dwarf feeling one bit of pain. All the people cheered.

"Now," said the dwarf, "not only am I the new king, but it is your turn to have the nuts cracked over your head."

The old king whimpered and wept so pathetically that the dwarf said, "Though you deserve this punishment, I am not nearly as cruel as you. And since you were once king, I shall honor that by giving you a very high post—in my opinion, the highest post." The old king went to his knees in gratitude.

"You shall be gardener," continued the dwarf, "and therefore feed your people well. And mothers shall bring their small children to play with you in the garden, and therefore you shall help raise your people well." The old king hung his head as if this were punishment. "And if you do not do your job well, I shall have to crack the cocoyole nuts over your head."

Fear rose in the old king's face. "But I do not know how to raise food or children," he complained.

"My mother shall teach you," said the dwarf.

And so it was that the old king ruled the garden and helped raise the people's children. And a curious thing happened. He began to smile and laugh, for at last he knew how to love and be loved.

As for the dwarf king, he ruled the people with kindness, wisdom, and fairness. Often at night he would visit with his mother and tell her the troubles of his people. She listened well and when asked, she gave advice, as any good mother would do.

The Fairy Man

It was, it was a fairy man
  Who came to town to-day;
"I'll make a cake for sixpence
  If you will pay, will pay."

I paid him with a sixpence,
  And with a penny too;
He made a cake of rainbows,
  And baked it in the dew.

The stars he caught for raisins,
  The sun for candied peel,
The moon he broke for spices
  And ground it on a wheel.
He stirred the cake with sunbeams,
  And mixed it faithfully
With all the happy wishings
  That come to you and me.

He iced it with a moonbeam,
  He patterned it with play,
And sprinkled it with star dust
  From off the Milky Way.

—Mary Gilmore
Australian, 1865–1962

Sir Buzz

Indian

nce there was a soldier who died, leaving a widow and one son. To add to their grief, the mother and son became so dreadfully poor that at last they had nothing left in the house to eat.

"Mother," the son said, "I have an idea. Give me four rupees and I will go out in the wide world to seek a fortune."

The mother cried, "Alas! Have you gone mad? Where am I, who haven't a coin to buy bread, going to find four rupees? What could you be thinking?"

"I was thinking about the pocket in father's old coat; perhaps you would find four rupees in it if you looked," replied the son.

So she looked, and lo and behold there were six rupees hidden away at the very bottom of the pocket!

"Ha! Even more than I had suspected!" said the son, laughing. "Here, Mother, these two rupees are for you to live on until I return. The rest I shall take with me to find my fortune."

So off he went, and on his way he saw a tigress licking her paw and moaning mournfully.

He was about to run away from the ferocious creature, when she called to him faintly, "Please, lad, if you will pull out this thorn, I would be forever grateful."

39

"No, I dare not," replied the lad, "for if I begin to pull it out, and it hurts you, you will kill me with one swipe of your paw!"

"No, I promise not to!" cried the tigress. "I will turn toward the tree, and when the pain comes, I will swipe that."

To this the soldier's son agreed. He pulled out the thorn, and when the pain came, the tigress gave the tree such a blow that the trunk split all to pieces. Then she turned to the lad and said gratefully, "I wish to reward your kindness. Take this box, but do not open it until you have traveled nine miles."

The soldier's son thanked the tigress, and set off again to seek his fortune. After five miles he was certain that the box felt heavier than it had at first. In fact, with every step he took it seemed that the box put on more weight! He struggled on with it until he had gone eight miles and a quarter—then his patience gave out altogether.

"This is a trick! That tigress must have been a witch!" he yelled. "I won't stand for this nonsense any longer. Wretched box! Heaven only knows what is inside you, and I no longer care!"

He flung the box down with such force that it burst open, and out stepped a little old man.

The man stood only one hand's span high, but his beard was a span and a quarter long, and trailed upon the ground. Perhaps that added some weight to the little fellow—one can never tell.

The little man immediately began to stamp about and scold the lad severely for putting the box down so violently.

"My word," exclaimed the soldier's son, trying hard not to smile at the silly little figure, "but you are a weighty soul for your size! And what might your name be, sir?"

"Sir Buzz!" snapped the little man, still stamping about in a fury.

"Well," said the lad, "if you are all that was in that box, I'm glad I didn't carry it any farther."

"That's not polite," snarled the little man. "Perhaps if you had carried it the full nine miles, you might have found something better. But that's neither here nor there. I'm good enough for you, anyhow, and will serve you faithfully as my mistress has instructed."

"If you are to serve me, by all means serve me with some dinner, for I am mighty hungry."

No sooner had the soldier's son said this than there was a great whirring and a whiz! boom! bing! like a bee as Sir Buzz flew off.

After some time the soldier's son began to wonder what had become of the little man when, whir! the small fellow alighted beside him, and wiping his face with a handkerchief, said thoughtfully, "I do hope I've brought enough. You men have such horrendous appetites!"

Looking at the huge sacks of food before him, the soldier's son laughed, "More than enough, I should think."

Sir Buzz cooked some griddle cakes and served the soldier's son three of them, while he himself ate seven more. Then the soldier's son ate a handful of sweets, and the little man gobbled up all the rest, exclaiming at each mouthful, "You men have such horrendous appetites, such horrendous appetites!"

After their meal they traveled a great distance until they reached the king's city. Now, the king had a daughter whose beauty equaled the most delicate of flowers, and her nature was as sweet as the most fragrant of blossoms; thus she was called Princess Blossom.

Now, by chance, or perhaps fate, the soldier's son caught a glimpse of the beautiful and sweet Princess Blossom, and of course, he fell desperately in love with her. He would neither sleep nor eat, and moped around all day long saying to his little servant, "Oh, dearest Sir Buzz; oh, kind Sir Buzz, carry me to the Princess Blossom so that I may talk to her."

"Hmph! Carry *you!*" snapped the little man. "You're ten times bigger than I am. You ought to carry *me!*"

Nevertheless, when the soldier's son grew thin and pale from pining away for the Princess Blossom, Sir Buzz was moved. He did have a kind heart, after all. And so he bade the lad to sit on his hand, and with a tremendous boom! bing! boom! they whizzed away and were in the palace in a moment.

They happened to arrive in the middle of the night, when the princess was sound asleep. The tremendous boom, however, awakened her, and when she saw the handsome stranger kneeling beside her, she opened her mouth to let out a scream. But the soldier's son begged her not to be alarmed. Then he poured forth such an elegant and polite speech that he set the princess at ease, and the two began to talk about everything delightful while Sir Buzz stood guard at the door.

Now, by the time dawn arrived, the soldier's son and Princess Blossom had fallen fast asleep. Sir Buzz was in a quandary. He said to himself, "Oh, dear me. If my master is caught here sleeping, he will be killed as sure as my name is Buzz; but if I wake him, ten to one he will refuse to leave. Now what shall I do?"

With little time left to think, he put his hand under the bed, and bing! boom! carried it into a large garden outside the town. There he set it

He poured forth such an elegant and polite speech that he set the princess at ease. . . .

down under the shade of the biggest tree, and pulling up the next biggest tree by the roots, little Sir Buzz flung it over his shoulder, and proceeded to march up and down like a sentry.

It was not long before the entire town was all in a commotion, for the princess was nowhere in sight. By and by the one-eyed chief constable came to the garden gate.

"What do you want here?" demanded the valiant Sir Buzz.

The chief constable, with his one eye, could see nothing but branches, but he replied staunchly, "I want the Princess Blossom!"

"I'll blossom you!" shrieked Sir Buzz, and with that he fiercely swatted the chief constable's horse with the branches until it bolted off, nearly throwing its rider.

The poor constable went straightaway to the king, saying, "Your majesty, I am certain your daughter is in the town garden, for there is an enchanted tree which fights ferociously and stubbornly refuses to release her."

Without further ado, the king summoned all his horses and soldiers to fight for the Princess Blossom. The men did the best that could be expected, but Sir Buzz managed to fend them off with severe blows of the branches.

The noise of the battle finally woke the young couple. They realized they could not exist apart, and so Princess Blossom came to a decision then and there. She made a stately announcement to all that were left standing that she no longer wished to live at the palace as their princess; she chose to marry the poor soldier's son instead. And so she did.

As soon as the ceremony was over, the soldier's son said to Sir Buzz, "Princess Blossom is all the fortune I need; my search is ended and I shan't need you anymore. You may go back to your mistress."

"Pooh!" said Sir Buzz. "Young people never think they need any help. However, have it your way, only take this hair from my beard, and if you should get into trouble, just burn it in a fire. In a wink I'll be there to help." With that said, he zoomed away.

The soldier's son and Princess Blossom traveled together happily, living on nothing but love and the four rupees from his father's pocket. Soon, though, they found themselves lost in a forest, and wandered about for some time without any food. A Brahman found them nearly starved to death, and said, "You poor children! Come home with me, and I will give you something to eat."

Now, had he said, "I will eat you," it would have been much nearer the truth, for he was no Brahman, but a dreadful vampire who loved to devour young men and women. But, of course, the young couple knew none of this, and went home with him as cheerfully as could be.

He was an especially polite host, saying to his guests, "Please, help yourselves, for I have no cook. Here are my keys; open all the cupboards but the one with the golden lock. In the meantime I will gather more wood for the fire."

So the Princess Blossom began to prepare a meal while the soldier's son went about opening all the cupboards. The more cupboards he opened, the more treasures he found: cups, platters, jewels and dresses, bags of gold and silver! His curiosity overtook him and he disregarded the Brahman's wish. He said to himself, "Surely there is something extraordinary inside the cupboard with the golden lock. I must find out." So he opened it up, but to his horror what he found were human skulls, picked clean and carefully polished. Hardly able to breathe, the soldier's son flew back to the Princess Blossom and blurted out, "We are lost! We are lost! This is no Brahman, but a vampire!"

Just at that moment they heard him at the door, and the princess, who was very brave and kept her wits about her, had barely time to thrust the magic hair into the fire, before the vampire appeared, baring his sharp teeth. At that selfsame moment a boom! boom! bing! noise was heard in the air. Whereupon the vampire, who knew quite well which enemy made that noise, turned himself into a heavy rain pouring down to drown the little man. But Sir Buzz was too quick for that trick and turned himself into a storm wind beating back the rain. Then the vampire changed into a dove and flew away, but he was pursued by Sir Buzz, who had changed into a hawk. He had almost descended upon his prey when the vampire changed into a rose and dropped into King Indra's lap as he sat in his celestial court listening to some girls singing. Then Sir Buzz, quick as ever, changed into an old musician, and standing beside the bard who was strumming the sitar, said, "Brother, you look tired; let *me* play."

And he played so exquisitely, and sang with such piercing sweetness that he brought tears to the eyes of King Indra, who said, "What can I give you as a reward? Name whatever you wish and it shall be yours."

Sir Buzz replied, "I only ask for the rose that is in your majesty's lap."

"Oh, I had rather you asked for something else," said King Indra, "it is but a rose, yet it fell from heaven. Nevertheless, it is yours."

So saying, the king tossed the rose toward Sir Buzz, but the petals fell in a shower to the ground. Sir Buzz tried to scoop them all up, but one petal escaped and changed into a mouse. In a flash Sir Buzz changed into a cat and gobbled up the mouse. And *that* was the end of the vampire!

Now, all this time the Princess Blossom and the soldier's son were wringing their hands, worrying what the outcome of the combat would be, when bing! boom! Sir Buzz appeared—victorious! He shook his head at the couple and said, "You two are not fit to take care of yourselves. I had better take you home." But first he gathered up all his enemy's treasures in one hand, and then with the other he took the princess and soldier's son and whizzed away to the lad's home, where his poor mother had been living on just two rupees for all this time. Needless to say, she was delighted to see her son *and* his good fortune.

Then with the loudest boom! bing! boom! ever heard, Sir Buzz, without even waiting for thanks, whisked out of sight and never was seen or heard of again—at least not by the soldier's son and the princess, for *they* lived happily ever after with little need of help.

Cradle-Song

From groves of spice,
O'er fields of rice,
Athwart the lotus-stream,
I bring for you,
Aglint with dew,
A little lovely dream.

Sweet, shut your eyes,
The wild fire-flies
Dance through the fairy neem;
From the poppy-bole
For you I stole
A little lovely dream.

Dear eyes, good-night,
In golden light
The stars around you gleam;
On you I press
With soft caress
A little lovely dream.

—Sarojini Naidu
Indian, 1879–1949

Little One Inch

Japanese

n the olden times in the little Japanese village of Naniwa, there lived a humble man and woman who loved each other dearly. They were quite happy with their life, but for one thing. They had never been blessed with a child.

Each day they went to a shrine and prayed earnestly for a tiny babe of their own, and one day they happened to say, "Oh, please, merciful one, give us a child. We want a child so very badly. We would be thankful even if it were no bigger than our thumbs."

Months went by and nothing happened, and then at last a child was born! The baby, however, was very tiny. In fact, he was only one inch tall—no bigger than their thumbs! So the couple named him Issun Boshi, "Little One Inch." And even though the boy did not grow any taller, the man and woman were still grateful and took loving care of him.

When fourteen years had gone by and Little One Inch had become a young man, he went before his parents. Bowing low he said, "Honorable Father, Honorable Mother, I thank you from the deepest place in my heart for caring so well for me all these years. I want to return your gift by making you proud of me. Grant me permission to go to the capital city so that I can become a great man and make our name known."

"But Little One Inch, the city is big and full of dangers, and you are so small!" cried his mother.

"Honorable Mother, give me then your sewing needle as a sword to protect myself, and I shall weave straw to make its scabbard," answered Little One Inch.

"And what shall you do for a boat?" asked his father. "The city of Kyoto is a long way down the river, and you are too small for a real boat."

"Honorable Father, give me then your rice bowl for my boat and a chopstick for my oar, and I shall paddle my way," answered Little One Inch.

His parents sighed, knowing that they must let Little One Inch go out into the great world on his own. So his mother handed him her best sewing needle and said, "This shall be your sword. Use it with great care."

Then his father handed him a painted rice bowl and chopstick and said, "And these shall be your boat and oar. Steer well, my son."

At the edge of the river Yodo, Little One Inch bowed very low, promising to return with honors. His parents smiled, but their hearts cried as they watched Little One Inch paddling away from them.

The big waves in the river Yodo thrashed the little wooden boat about, but Little One Inch was a strong boy and steered well. He soon reached calmer waters, only to find an unfriendly frog blocking his way.

"Frog, kindly move aside, if you please," said Little One Inch, but the frog did not oblige.

"CROOOAAAK!" it blurted out rudely, then grabbed the boat and began to shake it.

"I'll teach you some manners!" said Little One Inch. "I may be little, but I am strong." He spanked that frog with his tiny oar, and the surprised creature jumped off its lily pad and swiftly swam away.

Not long after, some large fish began to attack the strange-looking vessel, but luck was with Little One Inch. The wind came up and blew his boat across the water for miles and miles.

At last he reached Kyoto, the capital city. Little One Inch was astonished to see how big the city was. There were throngs of people dressed
in beautiful silk kimonos. There were flower girls, fine warriors, and large
carts pulled by oxen. Oh, the streets were crowded, and poor Little One
Inch had to dodge between all the many feet; for no one saw him at all.

Before sundown Little One Inch came to a very tall gateway which was
the entrance to a palace. It belonged to a famous lord of Kyoto. "Well,
this is the place for me," declared Little One Inch. "I shall see if I can
serve this great lord." And without any trouble he hopped through an
opening in the gate. He walked up to the enormous front door, and
standing beside a pair of fine shoes, he announced his arrival.

"Hello! Great lord, I am here!" But his voice was so thin that no one
heard him. He called out again, louder: "HELLO, I AM HERE!" Again
and again he called, until the lord, who happened to be on his way out the
door, heard him.

"Who is there?" the lord asked, looking all around him.

"Look down by your shoes!" called Little One Inch.

"Ho!" said the great lord. "What a tiny fellow you are. What is it you want, bean-sized boy?"

"I have come from Naniwa to serve you, great lord, so that I might learn to be as wise and great as you," said Little One Inch.

The lord was so delighted with Little One Inch's brave speech as well as his unusual size that he brought him into the palace to show his only daughter.

"You shall serve me by being her companion," said the lord.

"And her bodyguard," added Little One Inch, pointing proudly to the needle-sword by his side.

From that day forth Little One Inch was always at the side of the princess. They studied together, and he accompanied her to every event. They grew very fond of one another, and secretly in her heart the princess wished that Little One Inch were not so little.

One day the princess went to pray at a shrine outside the city. Upon her return an enormous monster, an oni, jumped out from the trees and grabbed the princess by the sleeve.

"Help me!" the trembling princess cried. But her frightened servants ran away, and there was no one to help her but Little One Inch.

"Let her go!" he yelled, "or you'll have to deal with me!"

The oni looked down at the ground where Little One Inch stood, and roared with laughter.

"So you laugh, do you? Well, perhaps you don't know me," said Little One Inch.

The oni swiped at Little One Inch, who promptly stabbed him in the hand with his needle-sword.

"Ouch!" exclaimed the oni, and swiped at Little One Inch again. But Little One Inch darted here and darted there, sticking the terrible oni in his toes and ankles and heels.

The oni hopped and danced about. At last he caught Little One Inch and was about to eat him up, when Little One Inch stuck him on the nose.

Ooo! That hurt the oni so much that he cried out, "Enough, enough! I humbly surrender." He set Little One Inch down and hobbled away.

The grateful princess ran over to Little One Inch and said, "You are braver than the bravest warrior! I thank you forever for saving me."

Little One Inch bowed.

Then the princess spotted something on the ground. "Look, Little One Inch!" she cried. "The oni left a magical wishing hammer! Perhaps he wasn't a monster after all, but a god sent in disguise to test you."

Little One Inch marveled at the hammer as the princess picked it up.

"If it is truly magical, it will give you a wish. What is it you wish for, Little One Inch?" she asked.

"I have nothing to wish for. I am serving a great lord and spending my days with you. Yet perhaps I wouldn't mind being a bit taller," said Little One Inch.

"Please, merciful one," the princess said quickly, "make Little One Inch taller." And she struck the hammer on the ground.

"Oh, oh!" cried Little One Inch, for the earth seemed to be rushing away from him. But of course it was just Little One Inch growing taller.

Repeating the wish, the princess struck the hammer again and Little One Inch grew some more. Then she whispered, "Make him grow as tall as a man." And she lifted the hammer above her head and brought it down with all her strength.

Standing now before the princess was Little One Inch, grown as tall as the tallest warrior! They both laughed joyously and danced all the way back to the palace.

There was a great feast held in honor of Little One Inch. All the warriors praised him for his bravery, and everyone marveled at his beauty, wisdom, and strength.

The lord of Kyoto announced that he would make Little One Inch a great lord. But first, he declared, the princess and Little One Inch would be married!

After the marriage ceremony, Little One Inch sailed off with his new bride to his parents' hut in Naniwa. His parents did not recognize the tall lord with the princess, until he bowed low to them and said, "Honorable Father, Honorable Mother, I have returned as promised." Then their tears of joy flowed like the river Yodo.

Soon Little One Inch and the princess brought his mother and father to their new home, where the old couple shared in their son's honors. And never did they stop giving thanks for the little one-inch son who had been born to them.

Ariel's Song

Where the bee sucks, there suck I,
In a cowslip's bell I lie;
There I couch when owls do cry.
On the bat's back I do fly
After summer merrily.
Merrily, merrily shall I live now,
Under the blossom that hangs on the bough.

— William Shakespeare

English, 1564–1616
Excerpt from The Tempest: *Act V, scene I*

The Moss-Green Princess

Southeast African / Swaziland

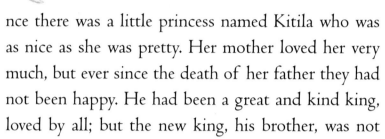

nce there was a little princess named Kitila who was as nice as she was pretty. Her mother loved her very much, but ever since the death of her father they had not been happy. He had been a great and kind king, loved by all; but the new king, his brother, was not so kind, and it was with him they now had to live. He made Kitila's mother one of his queens and Kitila one of his daughters, but he did not treat them well. In fact, he despised them and would not allow Kitila so much as one necklace of beads, and the little skin cloak she wore was shabby and not fit for such a princess as she.

The king had another queen, however, whom he did love, and together they had a pretty daughter named Mapindane. The king delighted in Mapindane's beauty and gave her many bead necklaces and fine skin robes, all befitting her charming ways. One might have thought there would be jealousy between the two princesses, but no; they played happily together, side by side.

Kitila's shabbiness did not stop anyone from admiring her. Perhaps they loved her all the more for that. The people's continued loyalty to Kitila outraged the king. He was afraid they would love her more than Mapindane, his own, true daughter—and this would weaken his power as the new king.

56

He was so filled with hate that at last he devised a cruel and hideous plan. Kitila would wear the skin of the Nya-Nya Bulembu, which would make her appear so ugly that everyone would be frightened of her and no prince would ever choose her for a bride.

Now, you may have heard of the Nya-Nya Bulembu. He is a strange, beastly creature who lives in the water. He has long teeth and claws and his skin is covered with bright green moss. Altogether, he is not a pretty sight and no one who can help it has anything to do with him. His very name means "the Despised One covered with Moss." The chief hoped that Kitila would be mistaken for the monster himself, and that everyone would hate her as much as he did. But he should have known better, for the Nya-Nya Bulembu is a faery beast and it is never wise to meddle with a faery of any kind.

The king called his bravest huntsmen together and told them of his plan. "Fetch me a Nya-Nya Bulembu," he said, "one that is young with all its teeth, long claws, and a perfect skin covered with green moss." He also ordered plenty of green mealie-bread to be made, in order to entice the creature out of the water.

The party of chosen men went down to the river and followed its course till they came to a deep pool, where the water was quite black. The huntsmen stood 'round in a ring and, holding out the mealie-bread, sang the song of the Nya-Nya Bulembu:

"Nya-Nya Bulembu, Nya-Nya Bulembu,
Come out of the water and eat!
The king has sent us for the great Nya-Nya Bulembu!
Come and let us see you!
Laugh and show us your teeth!"

Slowly a monster emerged from the dark water, but he was old, with only two teeth left and no moss on his skin at all.

"No," said the huntsmen quickly, "we don't want you."

They continued on until they came to a second big pool, which was as blue as the sky. So again they formed a ring and, holding out the mealie-bread, they sang the song.

Out came a vicious-looking beast with only a little moss on his coat and just three teeth, each two feet long.

"No, we don't want you either," said the huntsmen, and swiftly went on their way. They journeyed a long distance until at length they reached a third pool. It had the most beautiful fringe of green moss growing around it, and the water itself looked as green as fresh spring grass.

Once more the huntsmen sang the magical song and out of the water came a Nya-Nya Bulembu. Now, this one was covered with a nice thick layer of moss and showed all his long white teeth. Carefully they placed the mealie-bread on a rock before him, and when he came up to eat it, they caught him alive! Then they ran like the wind to the king's kraal. As they drew near, they cried out, "Have your spears ready, for here comes the Nya-Nya Bulembu!"

All the men in the kraal seized their spears and hurried to the gate. They stood in line at the entrance and when the green monster rushed toward them, he fell on their spears and died. Then the huntsmen took his body to the hut of the despised queen and her daughter, to prepare his skin as the king ordered.

When they opened the belly of the Bulembu, they were amazed to find the most lovely beadwork: necklaces, bracelets, and little embroidered bags of every color and pattern. Everything a princess could want was there, and it seemed that the more beads they pulled out the more they found, until there were enough to last a princess her lifetime. Kitila's mother was delighted, while Kitila looked on with curiosity, neither of them suspecting that it was the skin of the beast that was meant for Kitila and not the treasures within.

The huntsmen stripped the Bulembu most carefully, preserving the nails and all the teeth. And when the skin was ready, they took the little princess and wrapped her in it. The moment it touched her, it fit as perfectly as if she had grown it herself; indeed she could not take it off, for it was the skin of a faery beast, and this the king knew well. When the huntsmen looked at her, even they stepped back in fright, for it was the hideous green monster they saw now and not the little girl hidden inside the skin.

When Kitila and her mother wept at such an undeserved punishment, the chief councilor could only say, "It is the king's order; we must obey him."

Mapindane was the one child who would still play with Kitila, and so the two princesses sat by themselves near the cattle-kraal,

Mapindane was the one child who would still play with Kitila.

Mapindane wearing the beautiful beads of the Nya-Nya Bulembu and Ki-tila wearing his ugly skin. Still, the two little girls were great friends. As they played each day, hundreds of little birds came and the girls fed them, delighting in their company.

As the years passed, the little girls grew to be young women. Mapin-dane's loveliness brought pleasure to all who looked upon her, but poor Kitila, still dressed in the Bulembu's hideous skin, was as ugly as ever, and no one but her mother and Mapindane could bear to look at her.

There was to be a celebration of the first fruits of the harvest. The king's wise men had traveled to the sea to collect the water that would cleanse the land of all evil, and now everyone went out to gather the first fruits of the land. No one was left in the kraal but one old queen to watch over the two princesses.

The girls sat in their usual place, and the birds flew about them as they ate. Suddenly a flock of birds swooped down, seized Mapindane, and lifted her up into the air. Kitila cried after her, and the old queen looked up and shrieked, "There goes the beautiful princess. There goes the king's favorite child!" All the people came running from the fields, but there was nothing they could do. The birds rose higher and higher into the air and then flew north.

They carried Mapindane far away to another land and set her down in the kraal of a very great king. Poor Mapindane waited in fear, not know-ing what to expect, but then the king came to her and they fell in love at once. She married him and there she lived, happier than she had ever been. But she could never send a message home, for no one in her new land had heard the name of her people or knew the way through the thick forests that lay between them.

So Mapindane's father and mother never knew of her good fortune, and believed only that she had been eaten by the birds. And now poor Ki-tila in her green Bulembu's skin was worse off than ever, for the grieving king and queen were angry that it was *their* daughter who had been stolen and Kitila who was left alone. They no longer allowed Kitila to live as a princess, but made her do all sorts of degrading work. And no more could she be called Kitila but always Nya-Nya Bulembu. Often she said to her mother, "My life is so hard. Why was I ever born?"

But her mother always remembered that the Bulembu was a faery beast with magical powers and said, "Do not despair; everything will be right in the end."

Then Kitila went about her tasks with a lighter heart, and this the king could not stand. Finally he said, "What good are you? You are so ugly that even the birds fly away in fright. So go to the fields and scare away the birds. If you can't do that, then you have no worth to me at all."

Kitila wept, for she knew the birds were *not* afraid of her, and she would not be able to scare them away. But her mother said again, "Do not despair." And so she went to the fields, and there she met an old man. He gave her a stick, saying, "When you wave this in the air and shout, all the birds will leave the field at once. And when you go bathing, take the stick into the water and you will have your true shape again. But remember never to let go of the stick or the power will leave you."

Kitila thanked him and took the stick, wondering if the old man had been a faery in disguise. She soon found that he must have been, for every time she waved the stick in the air with a shout, the birds vanished from sight and she had no trouble keeping the crops safe.

In the hot afternoon, when everything was still and quiet and all the creatures were napping, Kitila went down to the river pool with her stick. As soon as her foot touched the water, the green skin floated away and hundreds of little faery girls came out to play with her. When they showed Kitila her true form reflected in the water, she laughed in delight at her own loveliness, and the faeries laughed with her.

Then Kitila stood in the water and sang:

She laughed in delight at her own loveliness, and the faeries laughed with her.

"Nya-Nya Bulembu, Nya-Nya Bulembu,
Here I am!
I was dressed like a monster,
But I am like any girl
Though they feed me with the dogs."

The faeries then brought her delicious food, and they all feasted and had a wonderful time together. But it did not last long, for when Kitila stepped out of the water, her green skin reappeared, and once again she was Nya-Nya Bulembu.

Now, all the little children were dreadfully afraid of the monster and never went near her. But there were two sisters who began to wonder where she disappeared to every afternoon. So one day, feeling a little bit brave, they secretly followed her to the river and hid behind a tree. When the children saw the monster's skin slip off and the beautiful girl appear, they were so astonished that they ran directly to Kitila's mother and told her all that they had seen. This brought great joy to the despised queen, but she told the children not to say a word to anyone. So the moss-green princess continued to scare the birds.

A few months passed and a great prince came to visit the king. He was handsome and young, but most of all he was wise. He had roamed many lands in search of a princess who was as beautiful on the inside as she was on the outside, but he had found no one whom he could love. At last he had come to the place where the moss-green princess lived. He went directly to the king and asked him if he had any daughters.

"Certainly I do," said the king. "I have only one, and you shall see her with pleasure."

"Yes, let the prince see the monster," said Mapindane's mother with a bitter laugh. So the prince was shown the way to the fields where the princess worked at scaring the birds, but to his horror he saw a hideous green monster walking about with a stick. He thought that he had been tricked and turned to go, but just then two small children came to him and said, "We will show you the princess. Soon she will be bathing in a secret pool in the river. Come with us."

They each took him by the hand and showed him which tree to hide behind. Soon the Nya-Nya Bulembu descended toward the river and again the prince was horrified and thought that he had been tricked. But he watched as the monster stepped into the water, and then to his amazement he saw the beautiful princess at last. He watched her play with the faeries, and he heard her sing of her sad life.

By this time the prince had fallen so in love with Kitila that he was ruled by his heart. He did not wait to see Kitila step out of the water and turn back into the Nya-Nya Bulembu, but went straight to the king and said, "I will marry your monster."

The king could hardly believe his ears and thought the prince must be dim-witted. But the thought of never having to look at Kitila again pleased him, and so he consented. All the wonderful gifts that the Bulembu had brought years before were now gathered together and were given to the young princess. The prince returned to his father and sent a present of one hundred cows to the king to show how highly he esteemed the young bride. He also sent a fine head of cattle for her mother.

Then he waited for the moss-green princess to arrive, for in that land the marriage ceremony is held at the bridegroom's home. All his people waited too, in great anticipation to see what beautiful bride their wise prince had chosen. You can imagine their horror when they saw the strange green monster arrive with long white teeth and claws, attended by four bridesmaids.

"How can this be?" they cried out. "This is the peerless beauty our wise prince has found? He is to marry a monster!"

The poor princess stood at the prince's door, trembling in fear lest he should realize his mistake and refuse her. But he kept to his bargain, despite her ugly green skin, and received her kindly. She was taken to a beautiful hut, where she would be prepared for her wedding the next day.

Very early the following morning, when the sun had barely shown itself, the princess and her maids went down to a pool in the river to bathe. Nya-Nya Bulembu held the stick in her hand and stepped into the cool river. As her foot touched the water, the green skin fell away, but this time it did not float as it had always done before. It rose up in the air and as it did so, a flock of birds swooped down and seized it. They carried it many miles until finally they dropped it at the door of the despised queen's hut.

When Kitila's mother saw it, she cried tears of joy, for now she knew that all was well and her daughter was happy at last.

The princess lightly stepped out of the water—never to be Nya-Nya Bulembu again but always Kitila, a king's daughter. She went to her hut, where her maids helped her dress in all her fine wedding array. When she walked out into the sunlight as her true self, the people were astonished. Never had they seen so lovely a princess, and no longer did they doubt the good judgment of their prince. And the prince smiled at Kitila, hardly able to contain his love for her.

The ceremony took place, and Kitila lived among the people in her new home in much happiness and honor. Word of her beauty spread far and wide so that people from the south, east, and west all came to see so splendid a woman.

As for the old king, he was forever punished. News of the beautiful princess soon reached his kraal. And while his people spoke of the well-deserved happiness of their Nya-Nya Bulembu, the king always believed his own daughter was dead, and never saw her again.

A Fairy Went A-Marketing

A fairy went a-marketing—
    She bought a little fish;
She put it in a crystal bowl
    Upon a golden dish.
An hour she sat in wonderment
    And watched its silver gleam,
And then she gently took it up
    And slipped it in a stream.

A fairy went a-marketing—
    She bought a coloured bird;
It sang the sweetest, shrillest song
    That ever she had heard.
She sat beside its painted cage
    And listened half the day,
And then she opened wide the door
    And let it fly away.

A fairy went a-marketing—
    She bought a winter gown
All stitched about with gossamer
    And lined with thistledown.
She wore it all the afternoon
    With prancing and delight,
Then gave it to a little frog
    To keep him warm at night.

A fairy went a-marketing—
    She bought a gentle mouse
To take her tiny messages,
    To keep her tiny house.
All day she kept its busy feet
    Pit-patting to and fro,
And then she kissed its silken ears,
    Thanked it, and let it go.

                    —Rose Fyleman
                    English, 1877–1957

The Elves and the Shoemaker

German

here once was a shoemaker who, through no fault of his own, had become very poor. At last he had only enough leather left to make one more pair of shoes. In the evening he cut out the shoes and placed the leather pieces on his table, intending to sew them the next morning. Then he and his wife said their prayers as usual and went to sleep.

The next morning the cobbler went to his table to work. He was just about to sit down, when he saw something he could not believe. He cried out in astonishment, and his wife came running in, expecting the worst.

"What is the matter, my dear?" she implored.

The shoemaker could not speak. He pointed to the table where his pieces of leather had been. There sat the shoes already finished for him! He picked them up to examine them more closely.

"Not one stitch is out of place," he murmured. "It's the most remarkable job I've ever seen; but who could have done this?"

"You need not look at me," said his wife. "I slept soundly beside you all night." They both scratched their heads, not knowing what to think.

Soon a customer came in. She was so pleased with the shoes, she paid more for them than the usual price. The shoemaker was now able to buy enough leather for two more pairs of shoes.

In the evening he cut them out and placed them on the table. The next morning he was all set to sew them, but there was no need to. This time *two* beautifully crafted pairs of shoes lay on the table, and with the money he made selling them, the shoemaker bought enough leather for four pairs of shoes.

Early the next morning the shoemaker went to his table and found *four* pairs of shoes, perfectly made; and so it went on. However many pairs of shoes the shoemaker cut out in the evening, that many were finished by morning. Soon he was no longer poor, but well-to-do.

Now, it happened that one evening not long before Christmas, the shoemaker said to his wife, "What if we were to stay up tonight and see who it is that is giving us a helping hand?"

The wife thought it was a wonderful idea. After the shoemaker had finished cutting out some shoes, they lit a candle and hid behind the curtain that hung in the corner of the room. There they waited.

At midnight two little elves, nearly naked, appeared. They took up the work cut out for them and with their tiny fingers and tiny tools began to nimbly sew and hammer. The cobbler and his wife could not tear their eyes away, so astonished were they. The elves did not stop until all their work was done. Then they sprang up and darted off.

The next morning the woman said, "Those little elves have done so much for us, I think we should show them how grateful we are. I feel sorry for them, running around with so little on; I am sure they must be cold. I would like to make them little shirts, vests, and trousers, and knit them each a cap and pair of stockings."

"And I shall be glad to make them each a pair of shoes," added the shoemaker. They stitched, knit, and cobbled all day, and late that evening, instead of laying cutout shoes on the table, they arranged all the little gifts they had made. Then the shoemaker and his wife hid again to see what the elves would do.

At midnight the elves came rushing in, ready to start work at once. But instead of finding leather cut out for them, they saw all the beautiful little articles of clothing. At first the elves were so surprised, they could not speak. Then they slipped on the clothing as quick as a wink. And with the utmost delight, they hopped and skipped and began to sing:

"Now that we're boys so fine to see
Cobblers no more we need to be!"

They danced 'round and 'round and leapt over the chairs and tables and ran right out the window. And from that moment on, they were never seen again in the shoemaker's shop; but the shoemaker and his wife did quite well as long as they lived, and were lucky in all that they pursued.

The Elf
and the
Dormouse

Under a toadstool
    Crept a wee Elf,
Out of the rain
    To shelter himself.

Under the toadstool,
    Sound asleep,
Sat a big Dormouse
    All in a heap.

Trembled the wee Elf,
    Frightened, and yet
Fearing to fly away
    Lest he got wet.

To the next shelter—
    Maybe a mile!
Sudden the wee Elf
    Smiled a wee smile.

Tugged till the toadstool
  Toppled in two.
Holding it over him,
  Gaily he flew.

Soon he was safe home,
  Dry as could be.
Soon woke the Dormouse—
  "Good gracious me!

"Where is my toadstool?"
  Loud he lamented.
And that's how umbrellas
  First were invented.

—Oliver Herford
English, 1863–1935

Laka and the Menehunes
Hawaiian

n the Hawaiian islands it is said that little people dwell in the mountains and hills. They peep and snicker at travelers who are passing by. Many can hear the hum of their voices, but only those who are true descendants of these little people can actually see them. It is also said that these little people, called Menehunes, have always been willing to do the bidding of their descendants, and their powers have enabled them to do some wonderful works, indeed; but they've also been known to do great mischief.

Once there was a young boy named Laka who lived on the island of Maui. His father so adored Laka that he would travel great distances to obtain a toy for his son. Hearing of a strange new plaything on the island of Hawaii, Laka's father sailed away to find it, but he did not return.

Years went by and Laka kept asking for his father, but his mother had no answer for him. "Go ask your grandmother," she finally said.

His grandmother replied, "Go to the mountains and look for the tree whose leaves are shaped like the moon on the night of Hilo; such a tree is for a canoe."

Laka followed her advice and rose early the next morning to travel to the mountains to find the tree for his canoe. At last he found the tree with crescent-shaped leaves and began chopping it. He worked all day, and by sundown he had felled the tree. Then he went home to rest; but when he returned the next morning, his tree was nowhere to be seen.

Determined to find his father, Laka began chopping another of the trees with crescent-shaped leaves. Again by sundown he had felled the tree and went home to rest. But once more, upon returning to that spot the next morning, he found the tree was gone. Laka was tricked this way for three days. But he did not give up his quest, nor did he lose patience. He resolved instead to catch the thieves.

Laka went to the mountains again, but before chopping down a tree, he dug a huge hole where it would fall. When he cut the tree, it fell right into the trench. Then Laka jumped in as well and hid.

As the moon rose, Laka heard a small humming and much giggling. Then, by the light of the moon, he could see a company of Menehunes.

"Let us raise the tree," said one, "and return it to its former place once again!" So, Laka thought, I have been chopping down the very same tree each time!

When they began to sing:

"E na Akua o ke kuabiwi nei,
I ka mauna,
I ke kualono,
I ka manowai la-e,
E-ibo!"

"O gods of these woods,
Of the mountain,
And the knoll,
At the water-dam,
Oh, come!"

Laka jumped out from his hiding place and grabbed two of the little men. The others ran away screaming. "I'll kill you for all the trouble you caused me!" he roared, though he did not intend to hurt them. Their tears and cries and the rapid beating of their little hearts stirred his pity.

"Don't kill us!" cried one. "If you do, nobody will be able to make you a canoe or carry it to the beach. But if you spare us, we'll gladly do it!"

Laka agreed and put the little men back on the earth, laughing as they scampered into the thicket.

True to their promise, they gathered their band that very night, and carved and hollowed the tree into the finest canoe ever to be seen on the island. Then, humming, they carried it to the ocean.

Laka was so overjoyed that he provided the Menehunes a great feast, which they ate in thankfulness. And when dawn came, they promised never to bother him again; and they all wished him well on his journey.

Laka's further adventures are a mystery, for they are not recorded; but if you ever go to that mountain, you can see for yourself the hollow he dug for the tree.

The Grouse

The grouse that lives on the moorland wide
Is filled with a most ridiculous pride;
He thinks that it all belongs to him
And every one else must obey his whim.
When the queer wee folk who live on the moors
Come joyfully leaping out of their doors
To frisk about on the warm sweet heather
Laughing and chattering all together,
He looks askance at their rollicking play
And calls to them in the angriest way:
"You're a feather-brained, foolish, frivolous pack,
Go back, you rascally imps, go back!"

But little enough they heed his shout;
Over the rocks they tumble about;
They chase each other over the ling;
They kick their heels in the heather and sing;
"Oho, Mr. Grouse, you'd best beware
Or some fine day, if you don't take care,
The witch who lives in the big brown bog
With a wise old weasel, a rat and a frog,
Will come a-capering over the fell
And put you under a horrible spell;
Your feathers will moult and your voice will crack—
Go back, you silly old bird, go back!"

—Rose Fyleman
English, 1877–1957

Tom Thumb

English

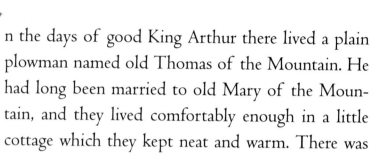

n the days of good King Arthur there lived a plain plowman named old Thomas of the Mountain. He had long been married to old Mary of the Mountain, and they lived comfortably enough in a little cottage which they kept neat and warm. There was nothing in their lives they could justly complain about, but for the one thing that was missing: a child.

One day the grief that old Thomas felt was so fierce, he could not contain himself, and he blurted out to Mary, "Oh, wife, I would be happy with just *one* child, one child even if it were no bigger than my thumb; a child of the very bigness of my thumb would bring me the greatest joy in the world."

He carried on in this manner until Mary said, "Enough! Do you not know I would do anything for such a child, and that I grieve too?"

Pleased by this, old Thomas said, "Then will you not go to the wise magician, Merlin, and tell him you wish to bear a child? Merlin is cunning in all arts, all sciences, secrets, and discoveries. He consorts with elves and fairies. He is a worker of night wonders, a commander of goblins . . ."

"Goblins!" cried old Mary, shaking. "I will have nothing to do with such a devil as he!"

"Did you not say you would do anything for a child? Well then, go to him, for he will tell you how to have one," said old Thomas. "And a good blessing a child would be, even if he were no bigger than my thumb."

Poor Mary, full of fear, wrapped a cloak around her and set out through the woods to find the old wizard. After a while she came to the dwelling of old Merlin, which was the hollow trunk of a blasted oak, all overgrown with withered moss and with wild animals lounging about the doorstep. Mary stood shivering in fright, about to knock upon the door, when it flew open of its own accord. And there was old Merlin sitting at tea with a diminutive person, a fairy lady, the Queen of Fairies herself.

They invited Mary to join them, and so she sat and told them all that her husband had instructed her to say, and perhaps a little more. Merlin smiled in amusement at the thought of a child no bigger than old Thomas's thumb. The Queen of Fairies too seemed pleased, and they looked at each other and winked. Merlin then lifted the lid off the teapot, letting the steam rise heavenward; and with a grave face he chanted:

"*Ere thrice the Moon her brightness change*
A well-formed child by wonder strange
By fairies' blessing he shall come
No bigger than thy husband's thumb!"

Mary's eyes widened as she watched the steam form into the shape of a tiny child.

Mary's eyes widened as she watched the steam form into the shape of a tiny child, before the Queen of Fairies quickly blew it back into the pot. Merlin once more covered the teapot and poured forth from it a cup of tea for Mary, as if nothing strange had happened. Gingerly Mary sipped the tea set before her, which, by the way, was more delicious than anything she had ever tasted.

After thanking them most kindly, Mary went on her way with a wonderful lightness in her heart.

And just as Merlin had promised, in three months' time old Mary gave birth. The Queen of Fairies arrived to help with the delivery, along with the elves and dryads, who served as her attendants. The child thus born had, the first minute it took life, grown to the size he would always be, and that was the very height of his father's thumb!

And so the child was named Tom Thumb by the Queen of Fairies, his godmother. She kissed him and called upon the other fairies to dress her little godson according to her orders:

"An oak-leaf hat he'll have for his crown;
His shirt of web by spiders spun,
With jacket wove of thistle's down;
His trousers be of feathers done.
His stockings, of apple rind, they tie
With eyelash from his mother's eye:
His shoes be made of mouse's skin
Tanned with the downy hair within."

Old Thomas and Mary were delighted, but it was a mistake of theirs to think that a little fellow such as he would also be of little trouble. For Tom Thumb was quite a handful—a handful of mischief, that is!

He was most cunning and full of tricks. When he played a game with the other boys, and had lost all of his own cherry-stones, he would sneak into their bags, take their cherry-stones, and again join the game.

One day, however, as he was crawling out of a bag of cherry-stones where he had been stealing as usual, the boy to whom it belonged happened to see him. "Ah, ah! my little Tommy," said the boy, "so I have caught you stealing my cherry-stones at last! Now you shall be punished for your thievish tricks!" With that, the boy drew the string tight around Tom's waist and gave the bag such a hearty shake that poor Tom was sadly bruised. "Stop! Stop!" he cried out. "I shall never steal nor cheat again; only stop that I may live to do good!" So Tom was released, and he did try to do good, but his curiosity sometimes overtook him.

Old Mary was once making a very special pudding and pleaded with her son to stay out of her way. But he was anxious to know just how this pudding was going to be made, and climbed up to the edge of the bowl. Unfortunately his foot slipped, and he plopped, head over ears, right into the thick batter. His mother, not noticing him, stirred poor Tom into the pudding-bag, and put him in the pot to boil. The batter filled Tom's mouth, preventing him from crying out; but when he felt the hot water, he kicked and struggled so much that the pudding rumbled and tumbled and appeared to his mother as if it were bewitched!

Just then a poor tinker came by begging for something to eat. Old Mary gladly gave him the entire pudding, which he put straightaway into the satchel on his back. He skipped off in a hurry, lest she change her mind. But the warm pudding rumbled and tumbled so upon his back that the frightened tinker, not knowing what to do, ran faster. Now it rumbled and tumbled all the more, and the tinker burped in fright.

By then Tom had cleared the pudding from his mouth and yelled out, "You, scallywag! Stop that burping and let me down!" The tinker thought it was surely the devil he heard on his back, so he threw the pudding down and ran away as fast as his shaking legs would carry him.

At last Tom, being free but covered with pudding batter, made his way home to his mother, who was by this time very worried about her son.

She rejoiced at his return and bathed him in a teacup. And to this day, all those puddings with the same roundness and thickness as that of poor Tom's mishap are called Tom Thumbs in his honor.

After the pudding adventure, Tom's mother was quite wary of all the dangers that could befall him; even the very wind seemed to threaten him. One day when Mary was to go milking, Tom begged to come along. So she carried him in the empty pail, then tied him to a thistle to keep the wind from blowing him away.

This was a mistake, however, for while she was milking one cow, the old red cow ambled over to the thistle bush and began to eat. Poor little Tom was tied fast and could not free himself in time before the cow took Tom and the thistle in one mouthful.

While the cow was chewing the thistle, Tom dodged its teeth and roared out, "Mother, Mother!"

"Where are you, Tommy, my dear Tommy?" his mother cried.

"Here, Mother," answered Tom, "in the red cow's mouth!"

Old Mary at once slapped the back of the red cow's head with one hand and with the other held out her apron pocket, catching little Tom as he flew out of the cow's mouth. Mary ran home with him, grateful that he had once more escaped a most dangerous predicament.

Again fearing for her son's life, Mary took precautions to keep him safe by locking him in the cupboard or keeping him in her pocket. But she knew this was no way for a boy to live, and so when Tom desired to help with his father's work, he was allowed to go.

His father set him in the horse's ear where he could be sheltered from the wind and sun. After some time Tom wanted a task to do. So his father gave him a piece of barley straw to use as a club for scaring away the crows from the fields. This he did most manfully, standing in the middle of the land and shouting, "Shoo, shoo, Crow, shoo," to keep the sown seeds from being eaten. But amongst the crows came a raven with poor eyesight. Mistaking Tom for a frog, it swooped down and seized him, carrying him miles away, with Tom all the while crying, "Shoo, Crow. Shoo!"

Old Thomas and Mary mourned the loss of their son. There was not a crow's nest nor a church steeple for miles that they did not search; but Tom was not to be found. Their grief was greater than when they had wanted a child, for now it was more than a child they longed for; it was their own Tom.

When the raven discovered that it was not a frog it carried in its claws but noisy Tom, it deposited him at the nearest resting point, which happened to be atop a castle wall. Tom nimbly ran along the wall and up the roof, where he looked down the chimney. Below he spied a giant, roasting meat. Poor Tom could see no way to escape; the walls were too high, and the sea lay beyond them. He looked at the giant again, but just then a gust of wind came and blew him down the chimney. And there stood Tom in front of the giant! He was frightened out of his wits, and ran with all his might to the nearest mousehole.

The giant was too slow to catch him, and roared out angrily, "Come hither, you imp! You little devil! You nothing of a man! You MOUSE!"

Now Tom Thumb, wishing neither to take up residence in a mouse's hole, nor to be called one, crept out to face what he must.

"I am not a mouse!" he retorted. "I am a greater man than you!"

Here the giant fell into laughter which shook the castle walls. Then, taking a good look at the little man, he said, "I am Gargantua. I can blow down church steeples with one breath. I can carry more than one hundred men. I can eat more than one hundred. I can kill more than one hundred. All this I can do; now tell me what wonders you can do."

"I can do more than this," said Tom Thumb, "for I can sail in an eggshell, which you cannot do. I can eat less than a wren, and so save food. I can drink less than a sparrow, therefore I am no drunkard. I cannot kill a rat with my own strength, and therefore I am no murderer. These qualities of mine are better than yours in the judgment of all folk, and therefore, great monster, I am better than you."

Gargantua was furious and grabbed Tom Thumb. He dropped him in his mouth and swallowed him whole, but Tom did such a jaunty jig in the

giant's belly that the monster grew queasy and stumbled out to the battlements and there spat Tom over the edge, where he fell down, down into the cold, dark sea.

Poor Tom surely would have drowned if a fish hadn't swallowed him up. And there he sat moaning, "Alas, from one belly to another. I do not like being eaten!"

Perhaps it was fairy luck that was with Tom, for in a very short time the fish was caught and brought to the castle of King Arthur.

When the fish was opened, everyone in the kitchen was amazed to find little Tom. They brought him at once to King Arthur, who was delighted.

In no time Tom became a great favorite at the court. He not only amused the king and queen with his merry dancing, nimble tricks, and funny stories, but he also impressed the Knights of the Round Table.

King Arthur took him along one day when he rode out on horseback. When it began to rain, Tom crawled into his majesty's vest pocket, and being thus settled close to the king's heart, he asked if he could please take leave to visit his dear old parents. The king agreed, and ordered a fine new suit of clothes for Tom and a mouse that he could ride.

Of butterfly's wings his shirt was made,
  His boots of chicken's hide;
And by a nimble fairy blade,
  Well learned in the tailoring trade,
His clothing was supplied.
  A needle dangled by his side;
A dapper mouse for him to ride,
  Thus strutted Tom in stately pride.

Upon his departing, King Arthur led Tom to his treasury and allowed him to help himself to as many coins as he could carry. So Tom took a silver three-penny piece upon his back, and traveled two days and two nights until he arrived with great weariness at his parents' cottage. They nearly fainted when they saw him, and so great was their happiness that all they could do was weep.

After they recovered, there was great rejoicing. Tom gave them the treasure he had painstakingly brought back, and told them of all his adventures. After a long visit he asked them to escort him back to the castle, which they did with great pride.

Things went well for Tom for some time, until one day the cook was missing a very important spice. The cook, himself, had misplaced it, but he blamed Tom, telling the king that Tom had stolen the cherished spice which flavored the king's favorite dish.

The king sent for Tom at once, but fearing his royal anger, Tom ran away and crept into a snail shell, where he lay for a long time until he was nearly starved. Then he spied a large butterfly and hopped upon its back. It flew with Tom from tree to tree while the nobility all chased after it, trying to snatch Tom. At last poor Tom fell from his seat and dropped right into a watering pot, in which he was almost drowned, except that it happened to be Merlin's watering pot, and the old wizard reached in and rescued him.

Tom was taken inside to dry off and warm up a bit, after which the butterfly fluttered in the open window, perched on Merlin's shoulder, and changed back into a fairy. She was the Fairy Queen's own daughter, and she had taken a great liking to Tom.

"You know you should not have run away like that," she scolded him.

"But they would have hanged me for stealing!" replied Tom, hardly able to speak, never having seen a young girl his size nor one so pretty.

"But you are innocent and should have told them so. Now, because you

And so the fairy changed herself into a butterfly once more and carried Tom back to the court.

have run away, they think you are guilty," said the fairy princess.

Tom smiled at her. "If you bring me back, I will face the king and his whole army, and I will tell them the truth—that I am innocent—come what may." And so the fairy changed herself into a butterfly once more and carried Tom back to the court.

King Arthur was overjoyed to see his Tom again and brought forth the spice, which he, himself, had found while searching the cupboards for proof of Tom's innocence. Nevertheless, he allowed Tom to stand and give a brave and moving speech in his own defense while the butterfly stayed by his side. Afterward King Arthur called for a ceremony to honor Tom as one of his Knights of the Round Table, and he ordered a special chair to be made upon which Tom could sit properly.

The Queen of Fairies summoned Tom's parents for the honorable event, and even Merlin came to watch the grand ceremony. Tom asked that the little fairy princess be at his side—and so she was and so she remained, for they were soon married.

And for the rest of his life Tom was known as the most loved of all the Knights of the Round Table.

Thus he at tilt and tournament
*   Was entertainèd so,*
That all the rest of Arthur's knights
*   Did him much pleasure show.*
With good Sir Lancelot du Lac,
*   Sir Tristram and Sir Guy,*
Yet none compared to brave Tom Thumb
*   In acts of chivalry.*

Minnie and Winnie

Minnie and Winnie slept in a shell,
Sleep, little ladies! And they slept well.

Pink was the shell within, silver without;
Sounds of the great sea wandered about.

Sleep, little ladies! Wake not soon!
Echo on echo dies to the moon.

Two bright stars peeped into the shell.
"What are they dreaming of? Who can tell?"

Started a green linnet out of the croft;
Wake, little ladies! The sun is aloft.

—Alfred, Lord Tennyson
English, 1809–1892

The Goblin's Cap

Korean

here was once a man in Korea who was quite proper in his worship of his ancestors. It was a custom to hold services for one's dead relatives and set out offerings of food and drink for them. The man went to great trouble to do this and was beside himself with joy to find that one day his offerings had been taken.

"See how our ancestors have enjoyed what we've served them," he said to his wife proudly. "Not one morsel of food is left."

His wife scratched her head, looking at the mess that had been left behind. "Were your ancestors this sloppy?" she asked.

"Oh, shush, shush," he said. "We must go and put out even more offerings for them."

Now, this continued for some time, until one day the wife complained. "We've been serving so many lavish feasts for our ancestors that we hardly have a thing left to eat ourselves!"

Her husband shook his head sadly. "Surely the spirits of our ancestors would not do this to us. They wouldn't want us to go hungry. Something is not right. Tonight we shall watch and see what is wrong."

So that night they hid themselves behind a screen by the altar and waited. The husband held tight to a long stick. Just past midnight they heard gruesome noises, burping and slobbering and the like. When they

93

peeked out, they could see the food disappearing—yet no one was there!

"Ah, I understand now," whispered the wife. "These are goblins, and they must be wearing the magic caps that make them invisible, the Ho-rang Gamte that my grandmother told me about."

The husband's face grew red with anger, and he raised his stick against the invisible goblins, but his wife stopped him. "Let us see if we can se-cretly knock off one of their caps," she whispered.

So from behind the screen they listened carefully to where the nearest goblin was gorging; and with a quick swipe of his stick, the husband man-aged to hit the goblin's head and knock off his cap. And there he was, plain as day. What a sight!

"Wheee!" cried the husband and wife gleefully, for it's always so excit-ing for a human to see a real goblin.

When the goblins heard them and saw that one of their members had lost his hat, they were terrified. They thought that demons worse than themselves were after them, and they ran away without looking back.

The husband and wife laughed and laughed, especially after the hus-band put on the magic cap and became invisible himself. They were hav-ing a great bit of fun with the cap, when suddenly the husband stopped. "Wife," he said, "fortune has fallen into our hands! We could use this cap to help us restore all that the goblins have taken from us."

The wife frowned. "What are you saying?"

"I could wear the hat and, well, just take enough things in the village to set us right again." He said this with a strange gleam in his eye, a ghoulish look his wife had never seen before.

His wife wrung her hands. "If everyone thought like you, there'd be no end to the wrongdoings in the world! Just because the goblins stole from us doesn't mean you should steal from others!"

But he would not listen to her, and at last she said, "I cannot be a part of this. That hat is evil. Look at what it's done to you already! I am

And there he was, plain as day. What a sight!

leaving." So she packed a few belongings and went to live by herself in a little hut on the hill.

The man seemed not to care. He put on the cap and went out to steal. He found that it was very easy. Money, jewels, and people's oldest treasures disappeared right before their eyes, and there was not a thing they could do. They blamed the thefts on evil spirits, when all along the culprit was their own neighbor.

"Ha! Soon my wife will change her tune, and beg to live with me again," he told himself as he filled his home with the villagers' goods. And each morning he exclaimed, "This shall be my last day of stealing, for after today I will have enough riches to retire." But he could not stop.

Now, as time went on, the goblins grew suspicious. They heard people blaming them for all sorts of thefts, when all they stole was food. They realized it must have been a human who stole their Horang Gamte, and they made plans to trick him.

They went to the house of one rich person after another, lying in wait from midnight to dawn, hoping to catch the thief. But they had no luck. As for the man, he kept stealing and stealing, never noticing that a red thread from the hat had begun to unravel from so much use.

One day the man went to the jeweller's shop. The jeweller was a sour, miserly man who cared only for his riches. He was carefully counting his money, when all at once he gasped. Stacks of coins were floating away from him! Then the opals and pearls started leaving their places, all on their own, or so it seemed to the jeweller. His knees shook as he searched the room for an explanation, for he was never one to believe in spirits of any sort. Then he saw a red thread moving through the air. He snatched it, pulling off the man's cap. And there stood the man, caught with his sack full of jewels and coins.

The jeweller angrily seized him and made the man return everything he had taken from him. The jeweller was about to turn the man in to the authorities, when the man fell to his knees and offered the jeweller the magic cap.

The jeweller did not have to think long. He took the cap, and let the man go.

The man felt as if a heavy weight had been lifted from him, and he ran up the hill to his wife. He begged her forgiveness, and forgiveness she agreed to give—if he would return all that he had stolen. With a remorseful heart, he did just that. His neighbors were overjoyed to have their treasures back and held no grievances against him.

The jeweller, on the other hand, left his business behind and went off to steal with his new magic cap. But this time the goblins were ready. They were waiting at the house of the wealthiest merchant in the village when the jeweller entered and began to steal things. The goblins grabbed their old cap and cried, "Wheee!" It's always so exciting for goblins to make trouble for humans, especially humans who do not believe in them.

A guard escorted the squirming jeweller out the door and straight to prison, where the goblins taunted him until he begged for mercy.

As for the husband and wife, they had just enough to live on and any extra they had they gave away to those who had run into misfortune. And from that time on they were always quick to tell their story of the goblin's cap to the village children, to warn them of the dangers of stealing. "For if humans do not discover you," said the husband and wife, shaking their fingers, "the goblins will."

hist whist

hist   whist
little ghostthings
tip-toe
twinkle-toe

little twitchy
witches and tingling
goblins
hob-a-nob   hob-a-nob

little hoppy happy
toad in tweeds
tweeds
little itchy mousies

with scuttling
eyes   rustle and run   and
hidehidehide
whisk

whisk   look out for the old woman
with the wart on her nose
what she'll do to yer
nobody knows

for she knows the devil   ooch
the devil   ouch
the devil
ach   the great

green
dancing
devil
devil

devil
devil

      wheeEEE

—e. e. cummings
American, 1894–1962

Vasilisa the Beautiful

Russian

nce there lived a merchant and his wife who had but one child, and that was a daughter they named Vasilisa. Everyone else called her "Vasilisa the Beautiful," for she was considered the loveliest girl in the village. But for all her beauty, she had a sad upbringing. When she was only eight years old, her mother became gravely ill.

Calling Vasilisa to her bedside, the woman whispered, "Listen well, Vasilisushka, and remember all that I tell you now. I am dying and can no longer be your mother. But do not fear, my child, I am leaving you with my blessing and this little doll." She lifted the coverlet and handed Vasilisa a little doll as beautiful as Vasilisa herself. "Always keep her with you," she said, "and never show her to anyone; if you get into trouble, give the doll food, and ask her advice. When she has eaten, she will tell you what to do." Her mother then kissed her daughter for the last time, and died.

The merchant mourned his wife's death and was terribly lonely. He began to think that marrying again would be good for his daughter's sake, and might ease his own pain. For his new bride he chose a widow who had two daughters of her own, thinking she would make a good mother for Vasilisa. He was quite mistaken, however.

Because Vasilisa was the most beautiful girl in the village, the stepmother and stepsisters were very jealous of her and tried to make her life

101

"Little doll," she would say, *"please listen to my troubles."*

miserable by giving her all sorts of difficult work to do. They hoped that she would grow thin and ragged from toiling so hard, and that the sun and wind would burn her skin.

Life was not easy for Vasilisa, but she bore her burden well. In truth, the work outdoors made her grow healthy and robust, while the stepmother and her daughters grew thin and ugly from sitting and complaining. But she could not have fared so well without the help of her magic doll.

At night, when everyone was asleep, Vasilisa would lock herself in her room and give her doll something to eat. "Little doll," she would say, "please listen to my troubles. I live in my father's house, but I find no joy here. My stepmother and stepsisters work me so hard that I have no rest and can barely stand. Tell me what to do." The little doll would comfort Vasilisa and tell her that all would be well. "Get some sleep now, Vasilisa dear. Tomorrow will be a better day."

When Vasilisa awoke the next morning, she would find that the doll had done most of the chores, leaving the easiest ones for her. Vasilisa picked the vegetables from the garden that the doll had already weeded. She fed the chickens whose coop had already been cleaned. She carried in the wood that had been magically chopped. She had only to add the grain and vegetables to the water that was already boiling over the fire to make soup. And in this way Vasilisa's life became easier.

Several years went by, and Vasilisa was now old enough to marry. Many young men came by to woo her and asked the stepmother for her hand in marriage. But the stepmother always sent them away, yelling angrily, "Never will I give the youngest away before the elders!" She would then turn her anger on poor Vasilisa and beat her.

One day Vasilisa's father left home on a long trip to trade in faraway lands. Wasting no time, the stepmother moved to a smaller house at the edge of a thick forest. Deep within this forest was a glade, and in that

glade was a strange hut perched on huge chicken legs, and in that strange hut lived Baba Yaga, the dreadful witch. Baba Yaga disliked people and ate them as if they were chickens.

Knowing this, the stepmother repeatedly sent Vasilisa into the woods on errands, hoping she would never return. But Vasilisa always kept her little doll in her pocket along with the best morsels of her meal for the doll to eat. And each time Vasilisa was lost in the forest, the little doll showed her the way home and steered her far from Baba Yaga's hut.

Autumn came and the light of day grew shorter and shorter. One evening the stepmother gave a task to each of the three maidens: The oldest was to make lace, the second had to knit stockings, and Vasilisa had to spin; and each was told to finish her task that very night. The stepmother snuffed out the candles all over the house, leaving only one candle lit in the room where the girls worked. Then she went to bed.

The girls worked awhile, and when the candle began to smoke, the oldest stepsister took her scissors to trim it. But she snuffed it out instead, for her mother had instructed her to do so.

"Oh dear, look what has happened! Now what are we going to do?" exclaimed the oldest stepsister, pretending that it was an accident.

"There is no light in the house and our tasks are not finished. Someone must run to Baba Yaga and get some light," said the youngest stepsister, going along with the plan.

"The pins on my lace give *me* enough light. I shall not go," said the elder quickly.

"Neither shall I go," said the younger stepsister, who was making stockings; "my knitting needles give *me* light."

"Then YOU must go," both of them cried out at once to Vasilisa. "Go to Baba Yaga!" And they pushed their little stepsister out of the room.

"At least let me get my cloak and some food to take with me," replied Vasilisa, and went to her room. There she put the best part of her supper before her doll and said, "Please eat, my little doll, and help me in my gravest need." The doll ate the supper, and her eyes gleamed like two candles.

"Do not fear, Vasilisushka," she said. "Go where you are sent, only keep me with you at all times and no harm will come to you."

Vasilisa put the little doll back into her pocket and threw her cloak over her shoulders. After making the sign of the cross, she ventured into the deepest part of the forest.

With trembling legs she stumbled farther and farther into the darkness. Suddenly a horseman galloped past her. His face was white, he was dressed all in white, and his horse and its trappings were all white. And as he passed, daybreak came into the forest.

Breathing a sigh, Vasilisa walked on. Then all at once another horseman galloped past her. He was dressed in red, and his horse was red as well. As he passed, the sun began to rise.

Vasilisa walked the whole day until she came to the glade where Baba Yaga's hut stood. To her horror the fence posts around the hut were topped with human skulls, and each skull had empty staring eyes; the gate had human hands for bolts and a wide mouth with sharp teeth in place of a lock.

Vasilisa was paralyzed with fear and could not move from where she stood. Suddenly a third horseman galloped by. He was dressed all in black, and his horse was black. He rode up to Baba Yaga's door and then vanished as if the earth had swallowed him whole. At that moment the night came and all was dark again. Slowly the eyes of the many skulls on the fence posts began to gleam, shining brighter and brighter until the glade was as light as day. It was a terrifying sight to Vasilisa, and she would have run away if she had not been so numb with fear.

Soon a terrible noise resonated throughout the forest. The ground trembled, the trees creaked, and the dry leaves crackled. From out of the trees rode Baba Yaga in a mortar which she prodded along with a pestle. And with a broom she swept away the tracks that were left behind.

Baba Yaga whizzed up to the gate, stopped, sniffed the air, and cried out, "Fie, fie! I smell Russian flesh. Who is here?"

Vasilisa walked up fearfully to Baba Yaga, bowed low to her, and said, "It is I, Vasilisa, Grandma. My stepsisters sent me to you to fetch a light."

"Very good. I know them well. Before I give you a light, you shall stay and work for me awhile. If not, I shall eat you up!"

Baba Yaga turned to her gate and shouted, "Come unlocked, my bolts so strong! Open up, my gate so long!"

Baba Yaga rode in and Vasilisa followed behind. The gates closed shut and bolted as soon as they passed through. Just past the gate grew a birch tree, and its branches swung down as if to lash Vasilisa, but Baba Yaga said, "Do not touch this maiden, birch tree. It was I who brought her."

They came to the hut and there stood a growling dog who looked as if

he would bite Vasilisa, but Baba Yaga said, "Do not touch this maiden, Growler. It was I who brought her."

They continued through a passage and there they met an old scratcher-snatcher of a cat who made as if to scratch Vasilisa.

"Do not touch this maiden, you old scratcher-snatcher of a cat. It was I who brought her." Baba Yaga turned to the girl and added, "So you see, Vasilisa, it would be foolish to try to run away from me, for my cat would scratch you, my dog would bite you, my birch would lash you and put out your eyes, and my gate would not open and let you out."

Baba Yaga's hut was perched on its chicken legs, and Vasilisa could not find any stairs leading to the door. "Hut, squat down," commanded Baba Yaga, and the hut squatted down just as a hen would, and they entered.

Baba Yaga stretched out on a bench and said to Vasilisa, "I want to eat.

Serve me what you find in the oven." So Vasilisa brought her a pot of borsch, chickens, pigs, jugs of milk, cider, and mead, enough to feed ten. Baba Yaga ate and drank up everything, leaving Vasilisa only a bit of soup, a crust of bread, and one tiny piece of meat.

Then Baba Yaga made ready for bed and said, "Now, Vasilisa, take this sack of millet, and before morning pick over every seed. Make sure you take out all the black bits; for if you don't, I shall have to eat you up." With that said, Baba Yaga turned to the wall, fell asleep, and began to snore loudly.

Vasilisa put the food she had saved before her doll, saying, "Please eat, little doll, and hear my troubles. Baba Yaga has given me a very hard task to do, and she will eat me up if I fail to do it."

"Do not worry, Vasilisa dear. Say your prayers and get some sleep. Everything will be as she wants in the morning."

As soon as Vasilisa had fallen asleep, the doll called out, "Feathered friends, come and answer my call. You are needed, one and all."

And flocks of birds came flying in. They picked over the millet, seed by seed, and put the good seeds in a sack while the black bits went into the field. The sack was filled to the top and the job finished when the white horseman galloped past the gate. Day was dawning.

Baba Yaga awoke and asked, "Well, Vasilisa, is the task all finished?"

Smiling cheerfully by the stove, Vasilisa replied, "Yes, Grandma."

When Baba Yaga saw that it was true, she was furious, but there was nothing more she could say about it.

"Hmph!" she snorted. "I am off to hunt now. While I'm out, you must wash the linens, sweep the house, and make my dinner."

"Yes, Grandma."

"That is not all!" snapped Baba Yaga. "You shall take this sack hither. It's filled with peas and poppy seeds. Pick out the peas from the poppy seeds and put them in two separate piles. And mind, if you do not do all this before I return home this evening, I shall have to eat you up!"

Baba Yaga went into her yard and whistled. There came her mortar, pestle, and broom. She hopped into the mortar and rode out of the yard, swinging her pestle like a whip and sweeping the tracks away with her twisted broom.

Vasilisa took out a crust of bread. Giving it to her little doll, she said, "Please, little doll, eat and hear my troubles."

After listening to Vasilisa, the little doll told her to wash the linens and make the supper; the rest she would take care of. Then she called out in a merry little voice that rang like sweet chimes, "Furry friends, come and answer my call. You are needed, one and all!"

And swarms of mice came pattering in. In no time, they had finished their task. The little doll was sweeping the hut after them as Vasilisa came in from washing the linens.

"Oh, little doll, you are my savior once again!" exclaimed Vasilisa when she saw the two neat piles of peas and poppy seeds. Then the two joyously danced about the room.

"Now," said the little doll, "I will sit in your apron pocket and advise you on which spices to add to Baba Yaga's supper."

With the little doll's help, it was not very long before Vasilisa had Baba Yaga's supper all prepared. "Take a rest now, Vasilisushka," said the little doll, and crawled back into Vasilisa's dress pocket. But Vasilisa was too fidgety, and decided to go out and clean the yard too. When it was getting on toward evening, Vasilisa went back to the hut, which was now standing up on its chicken legs. "Squat, hut," commanded Vasilisa, and the hut squatted for her and she was able to enter. She set the table and waited for Baba Yaga's return.

The black horseman galloped past the gate, night fell, and the eyes of the skulls on the fence began to glow. The trees creaked, the dry leaves crackled, and Baba Yaga came riding home.

"Well, Vasilisa, is all the work that I have asked you to do completed?" Baba Yaga asked.

"Yes," replied Vasilisa proudly, "all that you have asked and more. I cleaned the yard as well."

"What!" screamed the enraged Baba Yaga, who was secretly pleased to find a reason to find fault with the girl. "I did NOT ask you to clean the yard! You shall suffer for this!"

Baba Yaga said no more about the matter, but ate her supper, not nearly as much as usual, though; she left Vasilisa a pie, pork, soup, and bread, so as to fatten her up. Baba Yaga made ready for bed and said to Vasilisa, "You must light the fire and keep it hot all night long so that it is ready for roasting in the morning." Without another word, she turned to the wall and began to snore.

Vasilisa could not eat. Instead she wept huge tears into her soup and wrung her hands with worry. Putting some bread before her doll she said, "Little doll, please eat, and hear my troubles. I did not do as Baba Yaga asked, and now she means to roast me in the morning!"

The little doll told her just what to do. Vasilisa lit a fire that would last a little while; then she gathered her supper and crept out to the alley. There she met the scratcher-snatcher of a cat, but he did not scratch her, for she fed him her pie. Then she crept through the yard and met the growling dog, but he did not bite her, for she gave him her pork. She ran through the yard by the birch, but it did not lash her nor put out her eyes, for she tied a ribbon from her hair around its branches. The gate remained shut until Vasilisa greased its hinges, and then it swung open.

Vasilisa grabbed one of the lit skulls on the fence post as her little doll instructed. "Its eyes shall light the way home for you and will be the light your stepsisters sent you for," said the little doll.

"But won't the three horsemen now be able to find me and bring me back?" asked Vasilisa anxiously.

"No," said the little doll. "The white horseman is the bright day. The red horseman is the golden sun, and the black horseman is the black night. They will not touch you."

Baba Yaga woke up early and saw that the fire had gone out and Vasilisa was gone. She rushed into the alley. "Scratcher-snatcher, did you scratch Vasilisa as she ran past?" she demanded.

And the cat replied, "No, not I. She gave me a pie, so I let her pass. Though I served you for ten years, Baba Yaga, you never gave me so much as a crust of bread."

Baba Yaga rushed into the yard. "Growler, did you bite Vasilisa?" she demanded of her dog.

And the dog replied, "No, not I. She gave me some pork, so I let her pass. For all the years I've served you, Baba Yaga, you never gave me so much as a bone."

"Birch tree, birch tree!" shouted Baba Yaga in a frenzy, "did you put out Vasilisa's eyes?"

And the birch tree replied, "No, not I. She bound my branches with a ribbon, so I let her pass. I have been growing here for ever so long, and you never even tied them with a string."

Baba Yaga ran to the gate. "Gate, gate!" she cried. "Surely you stayed shut so that Vasilisa could not escape?"

But the gate replied, "No, not I. She greased my hinges, so I let her pass. I served you for ten years, but you never even put water on them."

Baba Yaga flew into a terrible rage that sent thunder booming through the forest. She chased the dog and cat around the yard, trying to beat them, and then she kicked at the birch and gate until she was so exhausted that she forgot all about Vasilisa.

When Vasilisa reached home, she saw that there was still no light in the house. Her stepmother and stepsisters ran out and scolded her. "Why did you take so long? We have been without a light this whole time. Whatever light we bring in from our neighbors, it goes out the moment we enter the house. Perhaps yours will keep burning." They took the skull from Vasilisa and brought it into the house. Its glowing eyes fixed themselves on the stepmother and stepsisters, growing hotter and hotter, burning them. They tried to hide, but wherever they went, the eyes followed, until they were burned to ashes. Only Vasilisa was untouched by the fire.

That morning Vasilisa buried the skull and ashes in the ground. Not wishing to remain in the house, she locked it up and went to town. An old woman who had no family of her own let Vasilisa stay with her while she waited for her father to return.

After a bit Vasilisa grew bored and said to the old woman, "Grandmother, I need to keep my hands busy. If you will buy me the best flax you can find, I shall spin it for you." So the old woman bought some very fine flax, and Vasilisa busily worked away and spun so fine a yarn that it was as thin as a strand of her hair. Then it was ready to be woven into linen, but there was no loom with a comb fine enough for Vasilisa's yarn. So Vasilisa asked her doll for help, and the doll said, "Bring me an old comb, an old shuttle, and a horse's mane, and I will make a loom for you."

Vasilisa brought everything to the doll that she had asked for, and went to bed for the night. By morning the doll had built a wonderful loom for Vasilisa.

All winter Vasilisa wove the cloth. It was so fine that she could pull it through the eye of a needle. In the spring the cloth was finished, and Vasilisa said to the old woman, "Grandmother, sell this linen and keep the money for yourself."

The old woman looked at the linen and shook her head, exclaiming, "No, my sweet child! Such cloth is fit only for the tsar. I shall take it to the palace."

The old woman then took the cloth to the palace and walked back and forth beneath the windows. The tsar saw her and asked, "What is it you want, old woman?"

"Your majesty," she replied, "I have brought you some rare cloth, but I will show it to no one but you."

The tsar ordered the old woman to be brought up to him, and when he saw the linen, he was truly astounded.

"What price are you asking for it?" asked the tsar.

"It is priceless, your majesty. I have brought it as a present for you," she answered.

The tsar thanked the old woman and rewarded her with gifts from the palace. Then he ordered shirts to be made of the rare cloth. But neither seamstress nor tailor could be found to do such fine work. Finally the tsar summoned the old woman and said, "You know how to spin and weave such fine linen; surely you must know how to sew shirts of it."

"Oh, it was not I that spun and wove the linen, your majesty," said the old woman. "It was the maiden who lives with me."

"Then let *her* sew the shirts," ordered the tsar.

The old woman returned home and told Vasilisa what the tsar had said. Vasilisa smiled and went to her room to begin her work.

She sewed and sewed, barely stopping to eat or rest, until at last she had made one dozen marvelous shirts.

The old woman took them to the tsar while Vasilisa washed herself, combed her hair, dressed in her finest clothes, and waited by the window. Soon she saw a servant of the tsar enter the courtyard. The servant told her, "The tsar wishes to see the needlewoman who made his shirts. It is his desire to reward her with his own hands." And so Vasilisa was brought to the palace.

When the tsar saw her, he fell in love at once. "Ah, Vasilisa the Beautiful," said he, "now that I have seen you, I do not want you to ever leave me. Will you be my wife?"

Vasilisa could hardly speak, for she too had fallen in love. She agreed to marry the tsar and took her seat by his side, and the wedding ceremony took place that very day.

It was not long before Vasilisa's father returned home. He was happy to hear of his daughter's good fortune and came to live at the palace with her. Vasilisa took the old woman into her home too. And though Vasilisa was never in trouble or sorrow again, she often spoke to the doll in secret and carried her in the pocket that lay closest to her heart for as long as she lived.

Evening Shadows

The evening shadows now unfold
Their curtain o'er the lonely wold;
The night wind sighs with dreary moan,
And whispers over stock and stone.
Tramp, Tramp! the trolls come trooping, hark!
Across the moor to the deep woods dark.

—Erik Gustaf Geijer
Swedish, 1783–1847

Anna and the Tomten
Swedish

It is Christmas eve on the Swedish farm. The night is cold and still. All but one are asleep on the farm. All but one are dreaming. He stands, a lonely guard at the barnyard door, so small that his beard is sweeping the snow. So small that no one could fear him.

Now the little girl wakes, for she cannot sleep. A star is glittering through the windowpane, and the snow on the firs is gleaming. Then she remembers the old tomten, and now she is very worried. Who has put out the bowl of rice pudding, a Christmas gift for him? What will the little old elf think when he sees all the gifts beneath the tree but nothing for him by the hearth, when each night he has checked the locks, he has fed the fox, he has scratched the head of old Dobbin?

The others do not care. They laugh at her, for they do not believe the tomten is really there. But the little girl, Anna, knows he is only hiding during the day, for at night he does her chores too. Sometimes while she is sleeping, he is sweeping, sweeping the chickens' house. And every morning she sees his small tracks that lead from the barn to the house and back. Anna knows the tomten is there, and now she wants to thank him.

She tiptoes down the worn pine stairs, down to the kitchen cupboard. She fills a bowl with rice pudding, then sets the gift by the hearth with a spoon. She's about to turn and climb the stairs, when something catches her eye. There in the corner the moonlight has struck the white of the little man's hair.

The tomten stands at the windowsill, pondering an old riddle. He sighs and shakes his head to clear away his dizzy thoughts. "Nay, 'tis too hard, I fear. Maybe I will never know," he says with great sadness. He turns and sees the little girl.

So startled is the tomten that he jumps straight into the air and bumps his head on the ceiling beam.

Anna gasps. Happy to have seen him, yet afraid that he will run away, she dares not move.

He rubs his head. I should flee, he thinks. But then, I've never seen their eyes open before, and hers are so very blue. Perhaps it wouldn't hurt to talk to her. So he stirs the embers in the hearth and nods for her to sit. The little girl can hardly breathe. She trips on her nightgown and lands in the chair.

The tomten chuckles and so does she. "I need your help," he says. "I have an old riddle I cannot solve. The more I wonder, the harder it seems, and the heavier it grows on me."

"Tell me the riddle; maybe I'll know it," Anna urges the elf, and kneels close beside him.

" 'Tis this. Every night, year after year, I've come to do my chores. Many families have I seen in this house and many more I am sure to see. Babies become little girls and little girls grow into mothers. The mothers one day become grandmothers. Then, where do they go? Every year I am the same, but everyone around me changes. *Where* do the people go?" The old tomten shakes his head sadly and runs his hand through his shaggy white hair.

"They go to heaven," Anna says, pleased that she can help him. "Back to God, the One above who created us all."

"Heaven? God? But how do you know this?" the tomten asks.

"We know," says the girl, "because God gave us the baby Jesus, who

"They go to heaven," Anna says, pleased that she can help him.

grew to be a man and told us of the great circle of love. Then He returned to heaven, where we all may go when our chores are finally done. And tonight is Christmas, the night that baby Jesus was born a long, long time ago. We give each other gifts to remember all that He gave to us."

"Christmas," says the old tomten, nodding. "So that is what Christmas is." He spies the gift of rice pudding by the hearth. "Ah, you have remembered me as well." He smiles and leaps up. "Come, I'll play you a little tune I know. I'm so happy, I could dance on air!" But first the little tomten skips about the room sprinkling a magical dust so that no one else will awake. Then he takes his fiddle and bow and begins a merry tune.

Anna laughs, for she knows the tune, though she cannot remember how. Perhaps she heard it in a dream somewhere, but she does not know, and she does not care. She dances around the room, she and the tomten, leaping and laughing till they tumble to the floor.

The room is still. The little girl yawns. She gives the tomten a kiss good night, then climbs the stairs to bed. He waits until she is sound asleep before taking his fiddle and bow and putting them by the hearth, his Christmas gift for her.

The night is cold and still, and the snow on the firs is gleaming. All are asleep on the farm, all but the tomten are dreaming. He lies in his loft on the sweet-smelling hay and looks through the crack in the wall. One star shines like a jewel in the dark blue sky, and now its light shines from the tomten's eyes. The tomten smiles. His chores are done. He closes his eyes, and soon he too is dreaming.

The Little Old Man of the Barn

When all the big lads will be hunting the deer,
And no one for helping Old Callum comes near,
O who will be busy at threshing his corn?
Who will come in the night and be going at morn?

The Little Old Man of the Barn,
Yon Little Old Man—
A bodach forlorn will be threshing his corn,
The Little Old Man of the Barn.

When the peat will turn grey and the shadows fall deep,
And weary Old Callum is snoring asleep;
When yon plant by the door will keep fairies away,
And the horse-shoe sets witches a-wandering till day.

    The Little Old Man of the Barn,
    Yon Little Old Man—
    Will thresh with no light in the mouth of the
       night,
    The Little Old Man of the Barn.

For the bodach is strong though his hair is so grey,
He will never be weary when he goes away—
The bodach is wise—he's so wise, he's so dear—
When the lads are all gone, he will ever be near.

    The Little Old Man of the Barn,
    Yon Little Old Man—
    So tight and so braw he will bundle the
       straw—
    The Little Old Man of the Barn.

                    —Scottish Traditional,
            Collected by Donald A. Mackenzie, 1909

The Little Land

When at home alone I sit,
   And am very tired of it,
I have just to shut my eyes
To go sailing through the skies—
To go sailing far away
To the pleasant Land of Play;
To the fairy land afar
Where the Little People are;
Where the clover-tops are trees,
And the rain-pools are the seas,
And the leaves, like little ships,
Sail about on tiny trips;
And above the daisy tree
   Through the grasses,
High o'erhead the Bumble Bee
   Hums and passes.

In that forest to and fro
I can wander, I can go;
See the spider and the fly,
And the ants go marching by,
Carrying parcels with their feet
Down the green and grassy street.
I can in the sorrel sit
Where the ladybird alit.
I can climb the jointed grass;
   And on high

See the greater swallows pass
　　In the sky,
And the round sun rolling by
Heeding no such things as I.

Through that forest I can pass
Till, as in a looking-glass,
Humming fly and daisy tree
And my tiny self I see,
Painted very clear and neat
On the rain-pool at my feet.
Should a leaflet come to land
Drifting near to where I stand,
Straight I'll board that tiny boat
Round the rain-pool sea to float.

Little thoughtful creatures sit
On the grassy coasts of it;
Little things with lovely eyes
See me sailing with surprise.
Some are clad in armour green—
(These have sure to battle been!)—
Some are pied with ev'ry hue,
Black and crimson, gold and blue;
Some have wings and swift are gone;
But they all look kindly on.

 When my eyes I once again
 Open, and see all things plain:
High bare walls, great bare floor;
Great big knobs on drawer and door;
Great big people perched on chairs,
Stitching tucks and mending tears,
Each a hill that I could climb,
And talking nonsense all the time—
 O dear me,
 That I could be
A sailor on the rain-pool sea,
A climber in the clover tree,
And just come back, a sleepy-head,
Late at night to go to bed.

    —Robert Louis Stevenson
    Scottish, 1850–1894

 Afterword

In this collection I have had to make difficult decisions on when to preserve the specific language of the storytellers, and when I might take the liberty of embroidering by using my own language and, in some cases, varying the story line.

Hans Christian Andersen's "Thumbelina" is the only tale included in this book that was created (rather than retold) by a single author. I felt compelled to preserve his words as best I could, using the various translations I had gathered, including the oldest English version, Mary Howitt's 1846 translation.

Other stories in this collection are age-old folktales recorded by a specific author, such as T. Crofton Croker's story of Lusmore and the fairies, the Grimms' story of the elves and the shoemaker, and Steel's story of Sir Buzz. I generally preserved these stories and kept some of the authors' specific language.

The remainder of the stories had numerous sources with story lines that varied from one another; some sources were merely outlines. With these I took a storyteller's license to tell the tale my own way, preserving the elements that seemed essential to all versions.

The last story, "Anna and the Tomten," is largely my own, adapted from a poem called *Tomten* by the Swedish poet Abraham Viktor Rydberg (1828–1895). Swedish writer Astrid Lindgren also adapted the Rydberg poem in her picture book *The Tomten*. Lindgren, however, chose to emphasize the tomten's relationship with the animals on his nightly rounds rather than the riddle of life that perplexes the tomten in Rydberg's poem. I focused on the riddle—though I departed from the Rydberg poem in having the riddle solved before the tomten goes to sleep, setting the story on Christmas eve, and adding the character of the little girl.

From my Swedish neighbors in Minnesota, where I lived when I was young, I had heard the legend of the Jul Tomten, a Christmas tomten who is especially fond of rice pudding. I took all these sources and combined them, thinking that perhaps this was how one tomten learned of Christmas and became Jul Tomten— or, at least, was given an immortal soul.

Bibliography

General Sources

Arrowsmith, Nancy, with George Moorse. *A Field Guide to the Little People.* London: Pan Books/Macmillan, 1977.

Bettelheim, Bruno. *The Uses of Enchantment: The Meaning and Importance of Fairy Tales.* New York: Alfred A. Knopf, 1976.

Briggs, Katharine. *An Encyclopedia of Fairies.* New York: Pantheon/Random House, 1976. (Originally published as *A Dictionary of Fairies,* by Allen Lane, Penguin, London.)

————. *The Vanishing People: Fairy Lore and Legends.* New York: Pantheon, 1978.

Campbell, Joseph. *The Hero With a Thousand Faces.* Princeton, NJ: Princeton University Press, 1990.

Campbell, Joseph, with Bill Moyers. *The Power of Myth.* New York: Doubleday, 1988.

Clark, Stephen R. L. "How to Believe in Fairies." *Inquiry* (University of Liverpool) 30 (1987): 337-55.

Healy, Jane M. *Endangered Minds: Why Children Can't Think and What We Can Do About It.* New York: Simon and Schuster, 1990.

Keightley, Thomas. *The World Guide to Gnomes, Fairies, Elves, and Other Little People.* New York: Avenel Books, 1978.

Larkin, David, ed. *Fairies.* New York: Harry N. Abrams, 1978.

McHargue, Georgess. *The Impossible People: A History Natural and Unnatural of Beings Terrible and Wonderful.* New York: Holt, Rinehart and Winston, 1972.

Olness, Karen N. "Little People, Images, and Child Health." *American Journal of Clinical Hypnosis* (Minneapolis Children's Medical Center, University of Minnesota) 27, no. 3 (January 1985).

Pearce, Joseph Chilton. *Evolution's End: Claiming the Potential of Our Intelligence*. San Francisco: HarperCollins, 1992.

South, Malcolm, ed. *Mythical and Fabulous Creatures: A Sourcebook and Research Guide*. Westport, CT: Greenwood Press, 1987.

Steiner, Rudolph. "The Poetry and Meaning of Fairy Tales." Two lectures given in Berlin, December 26, 1908, and February 6, 1913. Translated from German by Ruth Pusch, published through the Anthroposophic Press, New York, and Rudolph Steiner Publications, London, 1942.

Yolen, Jane. *Touch Magic*. New York: Philomel, 1981.

Poetry

Allingham, William. *The Lepracaun*. In *Fairy and Folk Tales of Ireland*, edited by W. B. Yeats. New York: Collier/Macmillan, 1986.

Bangs, John Kendrick. *The Little Elf*. In *The Anthology of Children's Literature*, Third Revised Edition, edited by Edna Johnson, Evelyn R. Sickels, and Frances Clarke Sayers. Boston: Houghton Mifflin Co., 1959.

cummings, e. e. *hist whist*. In *Hist Whist and Other Poems for Children*, edited by George J. Firmage. New York: Liveright/W. W. Norton, 1983.

Davis, Katherine. *The Fairy Dance*. E. C. Schirmer Music Company, Boston.

Fyleman, Rose. *A Fairy Went A-Marketing; Fairies; The Grouse*. In *Fairies and Chimneys*. New York: George H. Doran Co., copyright 1920.

Geijer, Erik Gustaf. *Evening Shadows*. In *Scandinavian Folk and Fairy Tales*, edited by Claire Booss. New York: Avenel Books/Crown Publishers, 1984.

Gilmore, Mary. *The Fairy Man*. In *The Little World of Elves and Fairies*, edited by Ida Rentoul Outhwaite. North Ryde, NSW, Australia: Angus and Robertson Publishers, 1985.

Herford, Oliver. *The Elf and the Dormouse*. In *A Treasury of Verse for Little Children*, edited by M. G. Edgar. London: Bloomsbury Books, 1988.

Mackenzie, Donald A., comp. *The Little Old Man of the Barn*. In *Elves and Heroes*. Inverness, Scotland: Carruthers & Sons, 1909.

Naidu, Sarojini. *Cradle-Song*. In *The Sceptred Flute*. New York: Dodd, Mead, 1928.

Shakespeare, William. *Ariel's Song*. In *The Riverside Shakespeare*, edited by G. Blakemore Evans. Boston: Houghton Mifflin, 1974.

Stevenson, Robert Louis. *Fairy Bread; The Little Land*. In *Collected Poems*, edited by Janet Adam Smith. New York: Viking Press, 1971.

Tennyson, Alfred, Lord. *Minnie and Winnie*. In *The Home Book of Verse for Young Folks*, edited by Burton Egbert Stevenson. New York: Henry Holt, 1929.

Stories

Leelinau

Emerson, Ellen Russell. "Leelinau and Oskau, the Indian Dryad." In *Indian Myths*. Minneapolis: Ross & Haines, 1965.

Schoolcraft, Henry R. "Leelinau: A Chippewa Tale." In *The Myth of Hiawatha, and Other Oral Legends, Mythologic and Allegoric, of the North American Indians*. Philadelphia: J. B. Lippincott; London: Trubner & Co., 1856. Reprinted by Kraus Reprint Co., New York, 1971.

Skinner, Charles M. "Indian Mermaids and Fairies." In *American Myths & Legends, Vol. II*. Philadelphia: J. B. Lippincott, 1903.

Lusmore and the Fairies

Yeats, W. B., ed. "The Legend of Knockgrafton," as told by T. Crofton Croker. In *Fairy and Folk Tales of Ireland*. (Contains *Fairy and Folk Tales of the Irish Peasantry*, first published in 1888, and *Irish Fairy Tales*, first published in 1892.) New York: Collier Books/Macmillan, 1973.

Thumbelina

Andersen, Hans Christian. *Thumbeline*, translated by Richard and Clara Winston. New York: William Morrow, 1980.

Keigwin, R. P., trans. "Thumbelina." In *Hans Christian Andersen, Eighty Fairy Tales*. New York: Pantheon Books, 1976.

Lang, Andrew, comp. "Thumbelina" (1894 translation, probably by Alma Alleyne). In *Yellow Fairy Book*, edited by Brian Alderson. New York: Viking Press; London: Kestrel Books, 1980.

Opie, Iona and Peter, comps. "Tommelise" (first English translation by Mary Howitt from *Wonderful Stories for Children*, published in 1846). In *The Classic Fairy Tales*. New York: Oxford University Press, 1974.

The Dwarf of Uxmal

Bierhorst, John. "Building Mythologies: Adventures of the Hero." In *The Mythology of Mexico and Central America*. New York: William Morrow, 1990.

Shetterly, Susan Hand. *The Dwarf-Wizard of Uxmal*. New York: Atheneum, 1990.

Skinner, Charles M. "The Dwarf's House." In *Myths and Legends Beyond Our Borders*. Philadelphia: J. B. Lippincott, 1899.

Sir Buzz

Steel, Flora Annie. "Sir Buzz." In *Tales of the Punjab*. London: Macmillan, 1894.

Little One Inch

Haviland, Virginia, comp. "One-Inch Fellow." In *The Fairy Tale Treasury*. New York: Coward, McCann & Geoghegan, 1972.

Marmur, Mildred, trans. "The Story of Issoumbochi." In *Japanese Fairy Tales*. New York: Golden Press, 1960.

McCarthy, Ralph F., reteller. *The Inch-High Samurai*. Tokyo: Kodansha International, 1993.

O'Donnell, James E. "Tiny Finger." In *Japanese Folk Tales*. Caldwell, ID: Caxton Printers, 1958.

Sakade, Florence, ed. "Little One-Inch." In *Japanese Children's Favorite Stories*. Rutland, VT: Charles E. Tuttle Co., 1958.

Seki, Keigo, ed. "Little One Inch." In *Folktales of Japan*, translated by Robert J. Adams. Chicago: University of Chicago Press, 1963.

The Moss-Green Princess

Berger, Terry, adapter. "The Moss-Green Princess." In *Black Fairy Tales*. New York: Atheneum, 1969.

Bourhill, Mrs. E. J., and Mrs. J. B. Drake, collectors and arrangers. "Nya-Nya Bulembu; or, The Moss-Green Princess." In *Fairy Tales from South Africa*. London: Macmillan, 1910.

The Elves and the Shoemaker

Haviland, Virginia. "The Elves and the Shoemaker." In *Favorite Fairy Tales Told in Germany*. Boston: Little, Brown, 1959.

Hunt, Margaret, and James Stern, trans. "The Elves." In *The Complete Grimm's Fairy Tales*. New York: Pantheon Books, 1944, 1972.

Shub, Elizabeth, trans. "The Elves and the Shoemaker Whose Work They Did." In *About Wise Men and Simpletons: Twelve Tales from Grimm*. New York: Macmillan, 1971.

Laka and the Menehunes

Skinner, Charles M. "In the Pacific/The Little People." In *Myths and Legends of Our New Possessions & Protectorate*. Philadelphia: J. B. Lippincott, 1900.

Thrum, Thomas G., comp. "Stories of the Menehunes: Laka's Adventure." In *Hawaiian Folk Tales*. Chicago: A. C. McClurg & Co., 1907.

Tom Thumb

Jacobs, Joseph, comp. "The History of Tom Thumb." In *English Fairy Tales*. New York: Dover Publications, 1967. (Republication of the third edition, originally published by G. P. Putnam's Sons and David Nutt in 1898.)

Opie, Iona and Peter, comps. "The History of Tom Thumbe," 1621, from the Pierpont Morgan Library. In *The Classic Fairy Tales*. New York: Oxford University Press, 1974.

"Tom Thumb." In *The Golden Goose Book*. London and New York: Frederick Warne, first published 1904, reprinted 1976.

Watson, Richard Jesse, reteller and illustrator. *Tom Thumb*. San Diego: Harcourt Brace Jovanovich, Publishers, 1989.

The Goblin's Cap

Cole, Joanna, comp. "Hats to Disappear With." In *Best-loved Folktales of the World*. Garden City, NY: Doubleday, 1983.

Zong In-Sob, comp. and trans. "The Magic Cap." In *Folk Tales from Korea*. Elizabeth, NJ: Hollym International Corp., 1982.

Vasilisa the Beautiful

Guterman, Norbert, trans. From the collections of Aleksandr Afanas'ev. "Vasilisa the Beautiful." In *Russian Fairy Tales*. New York: Pantheon Books, 1945.

Whitney, Thomas P., trans. *Vasilisa the Beautiful*. New York: Macmillan, 1970.

Zheleznova, Irina, ed. *Vasilisa the Beautiful: Russian Fairy Tales*. Moscow: Progress Publishers, 1966.

Anna and the Tomten

Lindgren, Astrid, adapted from a poem by Viktor Rydberg. *The Tomten*. New York: Coward-McCann, 1979.

————, adapted from a poem by Karl-Erik Forsslund. *The Tomten and the Fox*. New York: Coward-McCann, 1966.

Lorenzen, Lilly. *Of Swedish Ways*. Includes Charles Wharton Stork's translation of "Tomten" by Viktor Rydberg. New York: Harper & Row, 1978.

Acknowledgments

Special thanks to Norman D. Stevens, Director of University Libraries Emeritus at the University of Connecticut in Storrs, CT, for his expert reading of the foreword.

I would also like to thank Cindy Kane for her astute editing and all her support, and my designer, Amelia Lau Carling, for her wonderful art direction. I appreciate the help of my models, Evie, Emmy, Rhys, Schuyler, John, and Donna. And I wish to express my gratitude to the people who helped me with my research: the many librarians both in New England and in New York, Norm Stevens, Robert D. San Souci, Ann and Ethel Olson, Betsey Biggs, Molly Beale, Victoria Wells, Celia Riahi, Elizabeth Moreland, Angela Brown-Burchett, and especially my husband, Dennis Nolan.

A Fairy Went A-Marketing, Fairies, and *The Grouse* from *Fairies and Chimneys* by Rose Fyleman (New York: George H. Doran Co., copyright 1920) appear by permission of the Society of Authors as the literary representative of the Estate of Rose Fyleman.

hist whist by e. e. cummings appears by permission of: MacGibbon & Kee, an imprint of HarperCollins Publishers Ltd, reprinted from *Complete Poems 1913–62* by e. e. cummings; and Liveright Publishing Corporation, reprinted from *Hist Whist and Other Poems for Children* by e. e. cummings, edited by George J. Firmage. Copyright © 1923, 1944, 1949, 1950, 1951, 1953, 1956, 1958, 1961 by e. e. cummings. Copyright © 1963 by Marion M. Cummings. Copyright © 1972, 1976, 1977, 1978, 1979, 1981, 1983 by the Trustees for the e. e. cummings Trust.

The author and publisher gratefully acknowledge permission to reprint *Cradle-Song* from *The Sceptred Flute* by Sarojini Naidu, published by Dodd, Mead & Company, Inc.

The Fairy Dance by Katherine Davis is used by permission of the E. C. Schirmer Music Company.

The Fairy Man by Mary Gilmore from *The Little World of Elves and Fairies* (Angus & Robertson, 1985) is used by permission of Angus & Robertson Publishers, a division of HarperCollins Publishers (Australia).

The Elf and the Dormouse by Oliver Herford is reprinted from *A Treasury of Verse for Little Children* selected by M. G. Edgar (London: Bloomsbury Books, 1988).

Index of Poems and Stories